THE MULTIPLE CHILD

By Andrée Chedid in English Translation

Andrée Chedid

THE MULTIPLE
CHILD

translated from the French

by

Judith Radke

LEE COUNTY LIBRARY
107 Hawkins Ave.
Sanford, N. C. 27330

MERCURY HOUSE
SAN FRANCISCO

© 1989 Flammarion (originally published as *L'Enfant multiple* by Editions Flammarion); English translation © 1995 Judith Radke.

Published in the United States by Mercury House, San Francisco, California, a nonprofit publishing company devoted to the free exchange of ideas and guided by a dedication to literary values.

This book is supported by a grant from the National Endowment for the Arts.

This is a work of fiction. Names, characters, places, and incidents either are the product of the author's imagination or are used fictitiously. Any resemblance to actual events, locales, or persons, living or dead, is entirely coincidental.

All rights reserved, including, without limitation, the right of the publisher to sell directly to end users of this and other Mercury House books. No part of this book may be reproduced in any form or by any electronic or mechanical means, including information storage and retrieval systems, without permission in writing from the publisher, except by a reviewer who may quote brief passages in a review.

United States Constitution, First Amendment: Congress shall make no law respecting an establishment of religion, or prohibiting the free exercise thereof; or abridging the freedom of speech, or of the press; or the right of the people peaceably to assemble, and to petition the Government for a redress of grievances.

Mercury House and colophon are registered trademarks of Mercury House, Incorporated.

Printed on recycled, acid-free paper and manufactured in the United States of America.

Library of Congress Cataloging-in-Publication Data

    Chedid, Andrée, 1920–
      [Enfant multiple. English]
      The multiple child / by Andrée Chedid ; translated by Judith
    Radke.
        p. cm.
      ISBN 1-56279-079-X
      I. Radke, Judith. II. Title.
    PQ2605.H4245E5413   1995
    843'.914—dc20   95–11059

                                          CIP

5 4 3 2 1
first edition

Child of our many wars
Multiple child
Child with a lucid eye
Who bears the burden of
A body always too new.

So the world goes round: Merry-go-round that time rules and history changes. Its fragile reins — liberty's reins—are still in our hands, however, guiding our temporary steed off its track toward our singular destiny.

To Charlot
from laughter to tears
from tears to laughter.

For Lorette Kher,
to the sun of life.

THE MULTIPLE CHILD

Walk through Paris one August morning on your way to work. Discover Paris as it comes out of its night; watch it gradually emerge from the developer fluid. Moisten your eyes with this city. Bless the fate that makes you a part of it. Surprise it, in its captivating nudity crossed by only a few passersby. Once in a while, stay on the edge of the sidewalk, count to twenty, thirty, forty . . . not a car in sight on the street. Wander along its avenues, weave your way through its many alleyways; go around its squares, walk beside the Seine, which takes on a copper glint, beside the trees that fill with light. Taste this silence that beats with the breath of so many. Feel it, face-to-face, charged with so many lives. Sing within. Savor.

That didn't happen to Maxime anymore. For quite a while now, the carousel's owner had had a glum look on his face as he went to his Merry-go-round, a sullen, world-weary pout that didn't fit his round face, his small laughing eyes under bushy eyebrows, his tuft of a mustache, his jolly bald-

4 ness. He accentuated the baldness by shaving the top of his head, keeping a crown of sparse brownish hair above his temples and at the nape of his neck.

Well over forty, he had either the flamboyance of an adolescent or a worried, thoughtful appearance, depending on his mood. More and more often, his usually debonair face was strained, swept with ripples of anger or filled with his fear of being taken for a fool. Because he'd grown pudgy —his barely average height made the change noticeable— Maxime Lineau had decided to walk to work at a fast pace. Uncle Leonard was the only one in the family of good height; he measured almost six feet; he was muscular, had a good head of hair. His nephew had always envied his athletic build, admired his robust temperament. Sometimes Maxime came across a jogger on the way. He pitied the oldest of them, their panting and their spindly legs. If they lifted their heads to greet him, they forced a rictuslike smile. He felt only irritation at the idea of adopting such foreign customs so blithely. He kept to his childhood habits, where sport was limited to soccer games in the commune school yard.

Except for trips to neighboring regions, the owner of the carousel had never traveled.

The luck that had smiled on him when he first set up his carousel had suddenly turned. The stock market was falling; speculators forecast the worst. Not conversant with the ins and outs of financial affairs, Maxime didn't own stocks or bonds; but the slump extended everywhere, even to his little business, a business to which he'd devoted himself for almost five years, and which he described as "artistic" in memory of his Uncle Leonard. Only he would have understood him. As soon as he had announced that he intended to leave his administrative job to get a Merry-go-round, his family had yelped. To leave a secure job to rush into such a dubious venture was, in their opinion, pure madness. "So you want to become an acrobat, do you? An acrobat!"

UNCLE LEONARD ASIDE, there had never been eccentrics in his family. All of them had kept "the outlandish fellow" at a distance, inviting him only to weddings and baptisms. During those celebrations, they encouraged him to entertain the group; they applauded him. His imitations, his clean-shaven gay face, his flowing, midlength hair floating behind fleshy earlobes fascinated little Maxime.

Totally devoid of resentment, Leonard pulled out all the stops. He had his nephew climb up on his shoulders, then he pranced, whinnying, around the banquet table, calling out witticisms to each guest.

From that height, faces merged in one eternal smile, neither reprimands nor threats rose to attack the child on his perch; he felt free, out of reach. Radiant. Torn between repeated bursts of affection for his uncle and his own more conformist nature, which drew him closer to other members of his tribe, going back and forth from one sort of behavior to another, Maxime was always unsure of where he stood.

Then suddenly a gap opened between him and his relatives. The word "acrobat" sparked, flared up under his skin; Maxime threw himself into his project just as he had long ago when he'd run after his kite as fast as he could go.

6   IN A BATHING SUIT, bare-chested, with feet ablaze, the child dashed over the fields. His long cord rose, stretched out toward the heavens, up to the giant insect, the many-colored bird cutting through the sky.

It was dawn, or else twilight, that imprecise and quiet time when things are more magical, adults less demanding. Light, free, fragile and quick, the kite—chosen, given by Leonard—pivots, pirouettes, hesitates, teases, turns out of the wind, catches it again. At the mercy of the dauntless toy, the child stops moving, takes off again, speeds up; he stops again, jumps in the air once more.

But one evening a ballet of passing birds came straight at the magnificent object, shattering its fragile frame, tearing its colored paper to shreds. One of them got caught in the cord. Its feet and wings could not work free of the delicate framework. The swallow and the kite wounded, gashed each other. Tangled together, they fell down at the boy's feet.

Shaken with sobs, moaning, he knelt, tried to gather up the scattered debris.

The next day he buried the feathered bird and the paper bird—you couldn't tell one from the other—under the same clump of dirt.

THE IDEA of owning a carousel got Maxime into action.

If only he were free of the yellowing walls, of his office manager's moods, of his ink-stained beechwood table, which tied him down for hours on end. If only he could abandon those files, those columns of figures, those names of persons unknown—and therefore of no interest to him. The idea of leaving it all enchanted him. He wouldn't even regret leaving the computers, which had appeared in the business a little while ago, and which he'd thought were marvelous at first.

On weekends, Maxime walked around his city to choose the site of his future carousel. He consulted, perused laws and codes, began to seek a license and a series of authorizations. In spite of difficulties, administrative steps to be taken, bank loan applications, and risks he would encounter, it was a happy time. In that period, Maxime was so in love with life that it, in turn, inspired his passion and gave him energy.

In anticipation, he imagined the revolving platform, its gleaming horses and gaudy cars. He exulted when he thought of the waves of children storming his future Merry-go-round. Although a confirmed bachelor and convinced he would never have children of his own, he was compensated by the delight...he would soon give children gaiety, pleasure, and sweets by way of compensation.

Maxime didn't lead a solitary life, however, and always managed; he didn't lack for company. Because he didn't consider himself very attractive physically, he was continually surprised that he could so easily coax, seduce so many different kinds of women, and he took constant satisfaction in his hasty conquests, his numerous adventures without commitment. He was glad he always met partners—often married women—who had a carefree attitude about love, and who didn't try to prolong their affair.

With Marie-Ange, a beautician in the Rue d'Aligre, things had almost taken a serious turn. They got control of themselves just in time; the husband was becoming more and more suspicious.

BEFORE SETTING UP the Merry-go-round, Maxime started to take a passionate interest in the history of the Place and bought a guide to the capital's monuments.

On this site, there had risen—in the Middle Ages—one of the most important churches in Paris, a starting point of the pilgrimages to Saint Jacques de Compostelle and often on the route of crusaders setting out to recapture the Holy Land.

In the fourteenth century, Nicholas Flamel, the "Alchemist," was a patron of the imposing edifice. Rumor had it that the man corresponded with other alchemists throughout the world, especially with Arabs from Seville and eastern Jews. They kept the secret of the philosophers' stone, which transmutes metals into gold. These mysterious and privileged links between Occidentals, Arabs, and Jews had made the Square a springboard between different civilizations for centuries, a secret zone of entente. Later, Maxime was to recall that fact.

The church was then rebuilt by Louis XII, later reinforced by Francis I. Destroyed by the Revolution in 1797, its tower, still standing, was bought by a demolition man who rented it to the armorer Dubois. The latter astutely dropped melted lead through a riddle, a kind of sieve, drop by drop, into wide vats. The business of making lead shot, which turned out to be profitable, enriched two generations of heirs.

Maxime supervised every detail of the construction of the Merry-go-round, chose each part of it. Trying to decorate it in "the old-fashioned way," he examined the quality of the wood, the silvering of the seven oval mirrors, the intertwining of the festoons, the roundness of the cupola—all with the greatest care. He decided on the colors of paint—one for the whole body, the other for the manes and feet—and he chose the coats for the horses: the thirteenth one would be white, with a copper mane, bridle, and feet. He decided to have only one car: a coach worthy of Puss in Boots, with two seats of crimson velvet. He demanded a perfect, trouble-free mechanism.

The government rented him a good-sized piece of ground at the southeast corner of the little square. This *forain,* that is to say, a small-time entrepreneur in a street fair, moved in, established himself, as if the little garden and its 170-foot tower were part of his inheritance from that day on.

At first, he walked around it with an owner's pride. He admired the restoration of the stones, stopped beneath the statues standing in their niches: the eagle of Saint John, the bull of Saint Luke, the lion of Saint Mark. Since 1871—he'd just learned this—the weather bureau had been using the Tower as an observatory, which you couldn't visit without permission. Now that his domain stretched out toward the stars, he considered himself in partnership with them and with the firmament.

The first two years were glorious. The *forain* was convinced that this place had waited and hoped for him and his Merry-go-round for all eternity. Everything succeeded at the outset. Little girls and boys flocked there, lots of money came in, his feminine conquests multiplied. No sooner did he have a yen for one of the women who brought children there, for a passing student, a neighborhood shopkeeper, than he immediately wound up with a date.

His family continued to ignore him; he didn't miss them. Thinking their behavior stupid and outdated, he was freed from Sunday obligations, as well as from those interminable meals on secular holidays or on holidays that were religious in name only.

IN THE THIRD YEAR, difficulties came along. His well-being evaporated little by little. The world depression spread; his debt became more burdensome. Irksome details and drudgery increased. Women became distant. The gradual disaffection of the children was the crowning blow.

The last six months had been particularly difficult. A tide of troubles swept in. Discouragement had taken hold of Maxime: he neglected his business; he didn't bother with his appearance.

When the turns of the Merry-go-round, as regular as a metronome, brought him face-to-face with one of the seven mirrors, it cast a pitiless image back at him. He was forty-four, looked ten years older. He had a heavy silhouette, his shoulders slumped; his black, moth-eaten pullover no longer hid his flabby potbelly. His cheeks were slack; his appealing baldness was taking on a waxen, lugubrious appearance. Even the looks women gave him were different: when their eyes met his, they remained dull, indifferent. On the other hand, Maxime garnered the solicitude and cooperative smiles of the old ladies. Their winks, their sympathetic words—seemingly an indication to him that they already considered him as old as they—made him shudder.

Now the *forain* covered his setup with a grayish tarp earlier and earlier, and left for his rooms in the Twelfth Arrondissement, worn out, disenchanted.

Now he took pains to make petty economies, which hardly got his business back on its feet. To reduce his energy bills, he no longer lit the lanterns; he didn't buy cassettes anymore, just put records on the turntable instead—the same old songs, long since gone from the list of top hits. He gave up hiring a helper on school holidays. He eliminated the little wooden sticks, the many rings hung from pieces of wood, and consequently the sweets handed out to the winners. That way, Maxime had the satisfaction of punishing children corrupted by television, of penalizing them—those "kids of today," who were more and more spoiled, less and less innocent. The circling dance of the Merry-go-round, its horses—eternally leaping—its carved coaches, didn't make *them* dream anymore! He congratulated himself regularly on not having any "brats."

Skimping, making do—as his family had always done, although their patrimony didn't seem to increase as a result—with his pinch-penny ways, he went back to a tradition of saving, of putting money aside for the future, which he hadn't cared about until now. Cutting back or going over figures roused in him ancestral habits that were reassuring. He became melancholy, embittered, parsimonious; his bitterness became a protective armor.

12   REVERTING to the other side of his nature—the more realistic, habit-ridden side—Maxime found himself telephoning his family to get an invitation. He went to their home one Sunday. The family's triumph was a modest one. But while the *forain* was giving all the details of his problems, telling the tale of his ruin, they suddenly bombarded him with advice and reproof:

"We warned you. Your Merry-go-round was your middle-aged fling. You'll have to get rid of it. Will you get your old position back? You're not old, but you're not so young either. These days, they take that into account . . ."

Maxime came around to their point of view. He would sell.

A producer of electric automobiles had just made him an offer. He made magnetized tracks for fairs and amusement parks; his Formula I was more and more popular. There were little multicolored bumper cars that collided in a burst of sparks and a deafening din. Music boomed from several sets of drums at the same time; a string of neon lights lit up, went out, at a hellish pace.

The buyer arrived to clinch the deal in a Ferrari with a chauffeur in a driver's cap, and headed for the little square, which was located at a very desirable intersection with lots of shops.

It was hot; the man took off his coat. He was wearing a salmon-colored silk shirt with a monogram embroidered on the pocket. He had manicured nails, horn-rimmed glasses. *He* wouldn't give Maxime a break. On the other hand, Maxime would try to get the best price he could for what he called only "a caprice, a hobby." He took a sudden dislike to the stupid wooden horses with their unchanging smiles, the exorbitantly priced coach with its peeling gilt. He turned away from the series of mirrors framed with garlands, which reflected the image of a loser. Maxime couldn't think of anything but getting rid of the Merry-go-round that had taken up five years of his life.

The argument with the buyer had been bitter. They hadn't reached an agreement. Coming out of the metro the next day, Maxime dragged his feet over to the Merry-go-round, grumbling all the while. He raised the heavy tarp, folded it back bit by bit, muttering at the thought he would have to dust all that paraphernalia, all those axles. At the end of his rounds, he uncovered the coach in exasperation.

There, inside it, he suddenly caught sight of a boy—hidden away, curled up on the red seat—a barefoot vagabond dozing away quietly.

Stupefied, then overwhelmed with an uncontrollable fury, the *forain* pounded on the door of the coach. He pulled it toward himself so violently that it almost came off in his hands.

"Get out, lousy kid! Out!" he howled.

Wakening with a start, the child straightened up, rubbed his eyes.

"'Out!' I said. Out!"

Under the fire of that rage, the angry cries, the boy was
petrified, on the alert.

"Out! Out!" thundered the voice.

Suffocating with anger, with nothing else to say, Maxime
shot his arm right into the coach and snatched the child by
his T-shirt. Tearing him off the bench, he pulled him over
the threshold of the gaping door, swung him over the platform; then, twice as strong in his exasperation, he sent the
barefoot boy flying through the air to land on the ground,
his wild hair on end.

The child staggered from the shock. He took one or two
steps to the side, waiting for his legs to stop shaking before
facing the *forain*. Then, he spoke, trying to keep the panic
out of his voice:

"I'd come to take a ride. There wasn't anyone here, so,
while I was waiting. . ."

"Who are you kidding?" cut in Maxime. "A ride? In the
middle of the night?"

His head straight, suddenly steady on his feet, his voice
calm again, the child took a step toward him.

"In our country, it's still night."

"Where's that—your country?"

The other froze again.

"You won't answer me?"

Maxime waited, getting his breath back. But, staring at
him with his faraway look, the child kept his lips tightly
sealed.

"I don't give a damn where you come from! I know that
in that getup, shoeless, looking like. . ."

Suddenly, right in the middle of his tirade, he noticed

16   that where the child's left arm should be there was only an empty space. Nothing but a swollen stump sticking out of his cotton shirt.

The *forain* stopped short, interrupting his abuse.

Old Joseph slipped the ring, set with a sand-colored scarab, on his grandson's ring finger.

"Your father's ring. It's yours. Always wear it. I had it made smaller to fit your finger."

Trying hard to smile, he hugged the child to him, caressing the nape of his neck. He couldn't bring himself to separate his own body from the boy's. Then he entrusted him to a friend passing through town. The friend was joining his family, which had been settled on the other side of the Mediterranean for several years. The two of them would take the same freighter to Cyprus. Then they would make it to Paris by sea or train, the cheapest way. The trip was to take five to seven days.

THE GARE DE LYON. Late May. Exactly noon.

A novice sun exploded in a sky that had spurned the beautiful spring season until now. It was spreading out, swarming over the city. It pierced the glass roofs of the hall;

it lit up the locomotives and railway cars, burnished the gleaming rails. With this sudden flare of light, even the memory of clouds and the ashen color with which they daubed faces and stones was fading away. Taking over from a moldy spring, the weather surpassed itself. It looked as if summer would win.

At the end of the arrival platform for the Marseilles train, Antoine and Rosie Mazzar—eyes peeled, hearts beating fast —were waiting for the child.

"Do you think we'll recognize our young cousin?" she asked.

The couple had been living in Paris for fifteen years, ever since the beginning of that indefinable war—both a civil war and one stirred up from without. Countless unfathomable conflicts immobilized their little country, shutting it up in a rattrap with no imaginable way out. Antoine and Rosie had never returned there.

With the modest inheritance of an old uncle—a naturalized citizen who emigrated in the last century—they were able to get a laundry. Both were pushing fifty. Their business was in good shape.

Formerly, in their native country, Rosie had been a saleslady in a gift store. Rosie—whose models were the society women whose outfits and receptions filled the pages of magazines—had had an improvident and frivolous youth. Antoine reproached her for her heedlessness and chic finery.

But when they arrived in France and they bought the store, she took on her role of boss confidently and with a sense of her responsibilities. Rosie changed her style. She wore a chignon spun with white hairs, which she refused to dye. She dressed in calf-length dresses in natural colors, dark stockings worn with flat-heeled shoes. Her husband noticed, with satisfaction, that she resembled the image of his mother more and more: devoted, a perfect cook, an organized manager.

He quickly turned away from his austere wife and became enamored of Claudette, a young woman, perched on spike heels, garbed in short, twirling skirts, adorned with clanking necklaces and long enameled pendants. She came to the shop two times a week. They turned over a batch of clothes to her—clothes of the laundry's clientele—that she took home for alterations and other requested work.

On the days she came, Antoine managed to stay close at hand. Tantalized by Claudette's presence, he couldn't hide his love. His wife became sullen; she tried not to show her irritation for fear of sending her husband into a rage. He had warned her right after the last checkup, when the doctor thought his blood pressure was too high, that from now on, he would have to go easy on his heart, which was vulnerable to stress and endangered by the slightest annoyance.

Rosie could bank only on the arrival of the little cousin to stop the slow erosion of their marriage. His presence would force Antoine to conduct himself like a serious parent, to guarantee the child a respectable atmosphere.

"We're sure to recognize him," Antoine answered his wife's question. "Since his birth, it's eleven years now, we've always had photos of him. Your cousin Annette saw to that!"

Leaving the train en masse, the crowd covered the platform. Packed together, they walked very quickly toward the exits. Rosie and Antoine were afraid they would miss the child's arrival, but he was looking for them as well. He wore a sign around his neck with the names of the Mazzar couple written in capital letters.

"Joseph! Joseph! Over here!" they shouted together when they caught sight of him.

The child got rid of the sign with a wave and rushed toward them.

"Aunt Rosie! Uncle Antoine!"

Suddenly, the couple stepped back, both at once, stunned.

The child too stopped short.

"Uncle Antoine? . . . Aunt Rosie? It's you?"

They had just noticed the stump sticking out of the short sleeve. The sight of that mutilated, incongruous thing turned their stomachs. They remained where they were, overwhelmed, motionless, with nothing to say.

The child, who had just understood the reason for their withdrawal, stepped forward to meet them. Reaching up on tiptoe, he stretched out his good arm, put it around the woman's neck, then the man's, pulling them—first one, then the other—toward him to kiss them.

Rosie had just enough time to whisper in Antoine's ear, "The old man could have let us know . . ."

But suddenly ashamed of her own repulsion, she leaned over and drew the child to her breast. Acutely embarrassed, she hugged him more fervently. Then she kissed his hair, his cheeks, murmuring, "My child, dear child . . ."

Again, she felt something strange under her lips: an emptiness, a hollow, where the right cheekbone should have been. Without appearing to do so, she examined the place her mouth had just brushed against. The only thing that could have caused it was a bullet fragment; its extraction had left a noticeable scar, a dent.

It was still hell on the other side of the Mediterranean. What could they do about it? They tried not to think about it anymore.

Aside from these mutilations, the child was handsome. His dark hair was a helmet of tight curls cut close to a round head. He had a straight nose, quivering fine-drawn nostrils, eyes as black and shiny as olives. His shoulders were sturdy, wide, his legs muscled; he was the picture of health. His skin had absorbed large quantities of sun. His whole person shone with an indefinable brightness. This truncated body, this wounded face had left his soul unscathed and inde-structible, it seemed.

"My child, my child," Rosie kept saying.

On the verge of tears, she still pressed the boy to her, as if she were trying to push him into her womb, which had never borne a child. She was moved in all her being; she trembled with an emotion unknown to her before. Had she missed the pleasure of pouring out her maternal feelings so terribly? In the midst of the crowd filing past and the persis-tent racket of the station, two feet away from Antoine—who thought that time was passing very slowly—Rosie pro-longed her caresses, ran her fingers through the thick hair.

The child too felt comforted. The absence of his mother,

the softness of her arms came back to him. He had been living with his grandfather for a year.

"Joseph, my little Joseph!"

"I'm not Joseph," he murmured. "My name is Omar-Jo. Aunt Rosie, my name is Omar-Jo."

Overcome with emotion, she did not hear him. Rocking back and forth to her own words, she repeated the spellbinding refrain:

"My child, my baby, my Joseph, *chéri!* . . ."

This time, he slipped away from her embrace, stood right in front of his two cousins and declared in a clear voice: "My name is Omar-Jo. Omar, like my father. Jo, like my grandfather Joseph."

The passing of time and distance had erased past events. Rosie had just remembered that "unhappy marriage," as the family always called the union of "poor Cousin Annette." When she thought of it and of her strict religious convictions, she stiffened. Antoine, too—whose faith was only a kind of clan tradition—was annoyed. What dogma, what beliefs, what society were this child's, whom he was planning to take into his own family?

"What is your religion, son?"

"God's."

"What do you mean?"

"My mother's and my father's . . . all the other religions, if I knew what they were."

Rosie broke her silence: "You know very well that the true religion . . ."

"If God exists, . . ." the child went on.

"If God exists!" said Antoine in alarm. Antoine didn't fulfill his religious obligations, but his official religious affiliation—a Christian, son of the Roman Catholic Church—reassured him.

"If God exists," the child continued calmly, "he loves us all. He created the universe, the world, and mankind. He listens to all our voices."

Evoking God in the midst of these comings and goings, this racket, the rain suddenly coming down in sheets on the glass covering of the vaulted ceiling, seemed bizarre and out of place to the married couple.

"This is not the place to pronounce the Lord's name," declared Rosie. "Let's go home."

"God is everywhere," murmured the child, looking in vain for a sign of approval on one or the other of the faces.

His cousin had just taken him by his one hand and pulled him away, following her husband to the parking lot. Their relationship with the child appeared less harmonious than she had hoped. They would have to stand up to a nonbeliever.

THE COUPLE would soon leave their two-room apartment to move into a tower in the Thirteenth Arrondissement. The new apartment—picked out from a floor plan, bought on credit—would be more spacious than this. The child would have his own room there.

Omar-Jo took off his knapsack skillfully. He pulled out little bags of coriander, dried mint, cinnamon, Turkish-ground coffee, and even a bottle of arak rolled up in corrugated paper.

"Grandfather sends you all this!"

Rosie had prepared stuffed grape leaves with sheeps' feet, white cheese seasoned with olive oil, so that the child would feel at home. She had also made cakes filled with pistachios and sprinkled with sugar. He ate hungrily.

Omar-Jo served himself and manipulated his eating utensils with dexterity. He peeled a peach with his teeth, offered to do the dishes, then made coffee. "I'm used to making it, even with only one arm."

He referred frequently to the empty space in a very natural way, trying to put them at ease.

During dessert, he told tales about his village, about his life with his grandfather, whose home he had shared since the accident.

Would he talk about the tragic day? The day that had forced him to leave the city to take refuge in the mountains with old Joseph? Antoine and Rosie were eager to know the details, but they didn't dare immerse the child in the horror of those memories once again.

"We've enrolled you in school for the next term. It's not far away; you can walk there. Aunt Rosie will show you the neighborhood."

"Will you be able to manage?" she asked.

With a mischievous gesture, the lad took a pen out of Antoine's pocket, pulled a half-filled notebook out of his own pocket, and traced his name, in Arabic and in French, in beautiful calligraphy on a blank page.

After the meal, they presented the many family photos to him. They were arranged in different places, on little lace mats, in frames of varying sizes.

"Do you recognize yourself? Here you are in your mother's, Annette's, arms. There, with old Joseph. With your cousins Henri and Samir. With Cousin Leila. On your eighth birthday . . ."

His eyes searched for a picture of his father, Omar; he didn't find one anywhere.

Rosie blurted out rashly, "The day of the accident, it was your father who tried to cross the demarcation line, dragging your poor Annette along with him, wasn't it?"

The child did not speak. He seemed to be elsewhere, out of reach. Somehow or other, the evening came to an end.

For several weeks the city had been at peace again. The inhabitants were convinced once more that the troubles had come to an end, that the agreement was going to be upheld.

It was a Sunday afternoon. It was warm, it smelled of dust and of damp sea air.

Omar was wearing dark blue jeans, a beige checked shirt open at the collar. Annette had put on her summer dress with little orange flowers and three ruffles at the bottom of the skirt. She was bare legged; the nasturtium orange of the cloth shoes harmonized with the color of the flowers of her dress.

"How about taking a walk, Omar?" she suggested.

"Yes, let's take a walk."

They agreed, almost always. That gave Omar a feeling of well-being that diminished, deadened the scenes of violence in the world outside, one after the other, for more than twelve years.

The child remembered everything. At any given moment, he could relive the whole scene. At any second, as if it were truly happening, he could go back into the room flooded with sunlight that opens onto the narrow balcony, slip between his father and his mother, brush against them, rub against Annette's skirts, hang on Omar's shoulders, hear their voices, their laughter.

Listen to them laugh. In spite of the daily risks, dangers of every sort—even their civil status was imperiled—they laughed a lot together.

That morning, their faces—so very young, so close together—were reflected in the rectangular mirror of the living room. Omar had his arm around his wife's waist, then he was kissing her on the cheek.

Omar-Jo was crouching on the floor. He was drawing. He had chosen to stay at home.

"We'll bring back ice cream for you. What flavor do you want?"

"Chocolate. The big cone."

"The biggest!"

They disappeared hand in hand, leaving the door open behind them.

OMAR AND ANNETTE have to go down five floors; the building has no elevator. Omar-Jo hears their footsteps on the tile floor clearly. As they disappear, their rhythm picks up. He can see them taking the usual double jump over the last three steps before each landing. He imagines their running, their strides. You would think they thirst for movement,

28   drawn to the outside. They go faster and faster, not holding onto the railing, tumbling joyously down the floors, rushing to meet whatever waits for them.

OMAR-JO will always wonder why he suddenly threw down his colored pencils. For what reason did he run to the balcony to call down to them that he'd changed his mind, that now he wanted to join them?

"Hey! Hey! Papa, Mama, I'm coming."

They've left the threshold of the building. They hear his cry, see him, call back to him in turn.

"Hurry down. We're waiting for you."

His sandals in his hand, so he won't lose a second, he rushes to the stairs.

Once at the bottom of the stairs, Omar-Jo had squatted down to put on his sandals.

He put on one. Only one.

A violent explosion rent the air, followed by another blast that shook the whole building.

His second sandal in his hand, the child rushed outside.

Listen . . . ," the *forain* resumed, struggling to calm down, a short time after he had discovered the amputated child. "With bare feet and not a red cent to your name. I'd never have let you get on my carousel. Not at night, not during the day!"

"My shoes are in your coach," the child retorted. "You have to give them back to me."

That was too much to take.

"Get rid of them, you mean! And you with them! You and your lice, get out, clear out of here as fast as you can."

"Lice! I don't have any. I never have. Look."

He approached, shook his thick black hair, slipped his hand into the curls.

"Can you find even one?"

"Beat it, or I'm calling the police."

"The police! Why the police?"

The child stood erect, calm and confident in his posture. He had sized up the individual facing him in a glance. Behind his insults and irritability, the man seemed fragile,

30   sensitive to him, even compassionate. Because of all he had lived through in his ruined country, Omar-Jo, in spite of his young age, had acquired an accurate perception of human beings, an understanding of existence and its precariousness that made him clear sighted and patient.

"Why 'beat it!'? Why 'the police'? Why use those words with me? We could settle things, get along."

"Settle things? How do you expect us to settle things?"

Maxime, still on the ground beside the Merry-go-round, examined the boy. He tried to avoid the boy's eyes, which sought to meet his own gaze. In his mind, he associated him with those juvenile delinquents between six and fourteen years old who sneaked into the subway or department stores, with pickpockets who were capable of more harmful trafficking. "Criminal types," his family would have claimed.

Just because the kid had lost an arm didn't excuse everything! God knows what gang brawl or criminal mischief was going on when the accident had taken place.

"My shoes. I'd like my shoes back," demanded the child in a quiet voice. Maxime climbed on the carousel platform, went over to the coach—its door stood open—and spotted a pair of sneakers under the seat. Just as he was about to grab them, he stepped back, made a disgusted face, and bawled, "Come and get your dirty clodhoppers yourself!"

The child was only too willing. With one leap, he landed on the carousel, right next to Maxime. This time, the man noticed a square of patched skin above a hollow on the right cheekbone. The cheek had probably been pierced

by some kind of blade. This observation confirmed his suspicions: the youngster was probably part of a dangerous
band of hoodlums. Maxime was increasingly distrustful.

Meanwhile, the child had slipped on his sneakers, tied
the laces, still trying to look into the eyes of his companion.

"I don't have any money, but I want to reimburse you
for my night in your coach."

"Reimburse me? How?"

"Make use of me. You won't regret it."

"Use you? With only one arm, of what use could you
be?"

Without batting an eye, the child came back with "I'll
clean your Merry-go-round. I'll make a real jewel of it."

He waited a few moments before adding, "I offer you
all my services, gratis."

Feeling that he'd hit home, he insisted, "Do you hear
me?"

Maxime glanced toward the wooden booth where he
locked up the cash register; he always kept a small amount
of money there. Maybe the good-for-nothing had forced the
lock. He went over to it unobtrusively, moved the handle
several times. Everything seemed in order, intact.

The child, who understood the move, settled back on
his heels and suddenly turned the pockets of his knee-
length khaki trousers inside out. Their contents poured out
at the feet of the *forain:* chewing gum, a ballpoint Bic, three
colored pencils, a notebook, a pocketknife, small change, a
wadded handkerchief, four glass marbles.

"I didn't take anything of yours. I'm not a thief."

"That's good. Good," answered Maxime, ill at ease. "Pick up all that stuff and go away."

The child bent down, gathered up the small coins first, showed them to him. "They're not from here, they're from my country. They're not worth anything anymore, just souvenirs."

"Okay. Okay, . . ." grumbled the carousel proprietor, peeking at the foreign money; he couldn't make out where it came from.

The lad picked up the rest of it, then the four agate marbles that he spread out on his open palm.

"Choose. There's one for you."

"What'll I do with it? Go on, put it away."

"Haven't you ever played marbles?"

"Of course, sure I have."

"Well, do what I did, keep it as a souvenir."

Maxime carefully picked up the most brightly colored of the four, the one with orange and green colors twisted together in its center, with his thumb and index finger. It reminded him of his old marble, the one with which he always won.

Long ago, young Maxime used to collect little steel and glass marbles of different sizes in a glass jar.

At more than eighty years of age, Ferdinand Bellé would take him along in his tiny car to "do the shopping in town" and reward him each time with a marble when they got home.

Cutting short his wife's objections—she was twenty years younger than he and trembled at the sight of him at the steering-wheel—he left the cottage in Provence with its rounded tiles, accompanied by Maxime, the neighbor's son.

Shacks, made of poorly joined wooden boards or un-even stones, stuck like leeches to the narrow, ugly main building, extending it on each side. From a distance, the Bellés' home on the side of a hill looked like the tumble-down hovels of witches in the illustrations of children's sto-ries. The cottage with its odd-shaped forms looked out on Mont Saint-Victoire. "Cézanne's mountain," declared Denise, who had just retired from teaching.

34 As soon as he was in the car, old age left Ferdinand Bellé; the years fell from his shoulders. He didn't have to count on his legs to hold him up anymore; his eyes focused; his hands stopped shaking. He let the car rock him back and forth as they went down country roads. Then he took the turns on two wheels, possessed by a feeling of power that revived him, before he struck out on the freeway to join the lines of motorists following their exhilarating migratory instinct.

Back home, touching down, Ferdinand returned to reality and again took on the husk of an old man. His long spine stooped; his skinny fingers tapped the air uselessly; his trousers, which were too wide, fluttered about his phantom legs; his too-thin face seemed visible only in profile.

The last section of the path came to an end a few yards from the cottage. They had to abandon the vehicle, walk the rest of the way. The boy, loaded down with all the merchandise, climbed up the slope with the old man panting along behind him.

The reward was never long in coming, and the jar was soon filled to the brim. In order to use all his marbles, the child began practicing the games and was soon the undisputed champion.

A few years later, Ferdinand, still alive and a widower, continued to receive visits from Maxime. His passion for marbles had been replaced by a passion for bowls. Together, they joined the *pétanque* team of the nearby village.

Ferdinand was almost blind. Moving the *cochonnet* (the ball they aimed at), the players sometimes agreed to let him win. The old man accepted the applause with delight, never expressing doubts about his victory.

They were loving and joyful games, celebrated with drinks of pastis. The grasshoppers' song grew fainter and fainter. The mineral blue of the sky dissolved in the soft, luscious tints of the evening.

So," asked Omar-Jo. "What do you say to my proposition?"

His memory still filled with recollections of his own marbles, the *forain* put the one with the twist at its center, which he'd been holding in his fingers, in his pocket.

"What proposition?"

"You use me on your Merry-go-round."

Avoiding an answer, Maxime tried to find out more about the strange child. He pointed at the stump, then at the hollow high on his cheek.

"How did you get that?"

"An accident," answered the child, unwilling to confide.

"Are you part of a gang?"

Over there, gangs existed: mobile, dangerous, all of them armed. Gangs they couldn't catch, uncontrollable.

"I'm not a member of anything."

He had his own way of raising his head, not arrogantly, but as if to define his territory, to set its absolute limits.

"If I employ you, I have to know where you come from, don't I?"

"I don't ask you where you're from," the child retorted.

He stared at the other, lingering as he did every time their eyes met, trying to probe Maxime's gaze, and added, "A man who loves his carousel, I don't have to know where he's from. He's one of my family."

"Your family? Where did you get that idea?"

"Not my blood family, the other one. Sometimes that counts a lot more. You can choose it."

"You mean you chose me?"

"Yes, now I'm choosing you."

"It has to be reciprocal, don't you think?"

"It will be."

Times recently had been so grim, so depressing, that the carousel owner suddenly felt very pleased with this provocative exchange. He bent to the ground, bowed comically to the astounding child. "I'm flattered at your choice. Sincerely, very sincerely. Thank you, young man."

The child was helping him turn back the tarp, then stuff it into a wooden recess under the platform.

"Have you been hanging around here for a long time?"

"More than a month."

"I've never seen you."

"You don't see anybody, I've noticed."

"You were observing me?"

"Sometimes you have such a sad and tired look."

"You've never taken a ride on my Merry-go-round."

"Never."

"Don't you have any money?"

"Not at the moment, I don't."

"You've got a home, at least?"

"Not far from here."

"A family?"

"I live with cousins of my mother. They've been living in Paris for fifteen years."

"Do they have a resident card?"

"They're French. Naturalized."

"Good . . . but what about your parents?"

The child turned his head away; he still couldn't answer that question. If he were even to pronounce the names "Annette" and "Omar," he was certain his mouth would burst into flame.

"They abandoned you?"

The child stiffened; it almost took his breath away. "They never would have abandoned me."

Conscious of the distress he'd caused, the *forain* continued: "You can tell me about that later. Well, if you want to."

Before he could open the Merry-go-round, he had to tend to a number of tasks. Maxime went off to take care of them.

SEATED, his legs dangling over the edge of the carousel, the child contemplated the little Place, wondered about the enigmatic Tower, watched in anticipation for the first strollers to arrive on the scene. It was seven in the morning. Except for a few pigeons that moved about listlessly on the hard ground, the square was still deserted.

When the old woman arrived, with her wobbly steps, a heavy skirt, and mauve scarf, the atmosphere changed. She pulled a brown paper sack out of her shopping bag, emptied seeds from it, and scattered them over the ground, on her head, her shoulders, and her open palm.

Notified in some mysterious way of her presence, the pigeons, roused from their torpor, hurried from all directions, multiplying, fluttering, cooing, pecking. The woman looked like a vast perch sown with wings. Her sweet, crumpled little face seemed to grow smoother, blushing pink with pleasure.

At the same time, seated on one of the public benches, a young man was scribbling away in a notebook. All of a sudden, he would cross out his lines angrily, tear out a sheet, and throw it away. There were already a dozen of them wadded at his feet. Then he started over. Anxiety, increasing each time, cut deep creases in his forehead, clenched his jaw.

Finally, he got up. He paced nervously back and forth in the little garden before going to the gray stone lion set in a flower bed at the bottom of the Tower. The medieval statue looked like an enormous cat. He petted it for a long time between the ears, all the way down its spine, and with that familiar, sensory gesture, he seemed to find renewed energy. A few minutes later, he was back at his seat on the bench. He started to write excitedly, page after page, all of which he kept this time, tearing them from his notebook and stuffing them in his pockets as he went along.

Absorbed in their own affairs, as indifferent to their surroundings as they were to the vibrations of the city, which little by little was coming out of its inactivity, neither the young man nor the pigeon lady had caught a glimpse of each other.

Omar-Jo, though, had discovered everything. He had seen everything, thought about everything—all that had happened in and around the place, of which he was already a part. It seemed to him that the little Place—with its square, its cast of secondary characters, its Tower, its carousel—continued its autonomous existence on the edge of the city.

Then he looked farther away, toward the passersby coming out of the closest metro exit. There were more and more of them—all unaware of each other; they set off at a brisk pace toward their own destinations.

OMAR-JO STOOD UP, walked around the platform, placed his hand on the sculpted roof of the coach. After a few seconds, he said to Maxime, who was doing his best to patch a stirrup on one of the wooden horses:

"Your carousel is beautiful. But I'm the one who will make it the most beautiful in the whole country!"

Without waiting for an answer, the child went over to the booth, went in, rummaged around in a rusty chest, pulled out scraps of cloth and cleansers. He discovered a feather duster, a broom behind the cash drawer. Gathering them together, he came back to the platform and set to work immediately.

Going from the gray-spotted horse to the black, to the sorrel, to the cherry bay, he rubbed their legs, their chests, their flanks; he scrubbed them down as if they were alive. He made their manes gleam, their reins and bridles sparkle. Astride each mount, he rinsed out, then scraped their ears, their nostrils.

"Dust traps!" he exclaimed, a few feet from Maxime, who stared at him with his mouth open.

Last of all, he started to clean the coach. He swept the boards of the parquet, brushed the red-velvet bench on which he'd slept, dusted the wheels, polished the gilt. With bewildering dexterity, using his one arm, the child repaired the stirrup, made the seven mirrors shine.

At one and the same time himself and several others, he whirled about constantly from one place to another. It made Maxime dizzy! He closed his eyes, then opened them again, numerous times, wondering if he were delirious.

Suddenly, summoned by happy squeals, he spotted the child perched up on the roof, polishing the scarlet cupola.

"Get down, you're going to break your neck. If something happens to you, I'm the one they'll hold responsible."

"They'll see our roof from everywhere. Even from high in the sky."

"What a monkey you are!" yelled the *forain,* half scolding, half admiring, to the lad who'd just dropped down beside him.

"Clever as a monkey, you mean," shot back the child, immediately turning the expression into a complimentary one.

"That's it: 'Clever as a monkey!' You have an answer for everything. All right, perhaps now you'll agree to answer my question."

hat question do you want me to answer?"

"What's your name?"

"My name is Omar-Jo."

"Omar-Jo? Those two names don't go together."

"My name is Omar-Jo," the child insisted.

"That doesn't make any sense. None at all."

"It's my name."

"I'll call you Joseph. Or else, Jo—if you like that better. It's short for Joseph, everybody will recognize that."

"Don't mess with my name." His voice was curt.

In spite of the boy's playfulness, Maxime realized he could suddenly put up a wall of resistance to whatever offended him.

"I wasn't trying to annoy you."

"My name is Omar-Jo," he repeated more softly. "Omar and Jo: together."

"Omar-Jo," agreed the other.

"If you wanted to, you could add a third name to those two."

"A third name? What?"

"I'll explain later."

"Later," thought Maxime. "Lord, he's moving in. He's already right at home." The *forain* recognized that things were already set up, that from now on the carousel couldn't get along without the shrewd youngster.

"All my services: gratis. GRATIS," Omar-Jo sang to himself.

He put brooms, rags, cleansers back in their places and, coming back toward Maxime, said, "I'll put on a show for you!"

"A show?"

Without giving Maxime time to react, he rushed into the cubbyhole again. Squeezed in between the record player, the cash register, and an accumulation of odds and ends, he decked himself out in whatever came to hand. Then, scraping out the leftover paint in a few pots, he put on his makeup.

Maxime, who was watching him through the glass of the booth was slightly suspicious again, but he dismissed the thought. Troubled by contradictory feelings since the child had turned up, he wavered between distrust and sympathy.

He went to get a garden chair, came back, and sat down facing the Merry-go-round to wait for the unusual child. Curiosity, the spectator's impatience before the curtain goes up got the better of him.

The record player started to turn. A happy syncopated music announced the youngster's entrance. Omar-Jo presented himself: orange hair, cheeks of many colors, scarlet eyelids and mouth, the feather duster tied where his miss-

ing arm should be—all made him look like a bizarre creature—half-bird, half-human.

He strolled among the figures of the Merry-go-round,
smacked a kiss on the muzzle of the sorrel horse, mounted
another, stood up to full height on the saddle. Several times,
he entered the coach, came out of it, playing, in turn, a
monarch or a lackey, a lord or a beggar.

The whole place came to life. Maxime recollected his
past enthusiasms, his first excitement.

"Look at me!"

The child jumped down on the hard-packed ground
with his feet together, came forward to the *forain*, went
around his seat, his feet at right angles, swinging his hips
slightly. He made twirling motions in space with his invisible
cane, tipped his absent hat, put it back, lapped the air with
tiny licks.

Maxime burst out laughing.

"What a clown!"

"I don't remind you of anyone?"

The boy insisted, displaying the missing cane and hat,
turning out his toes, finally falling flat on his back, his legs
pedaling in the air.

"Chaplin! Chaplin! Chaplin!" exclaimed Maxime.

"Bravo! You've got it."

"What?"

"Omar-Jo Chaplin."

"Omar-Jo Chaplin? You're not serious?"

"Serious as can be."

Since he was a very little boy, he had worshiped
Chaplin, ill-treated by men and events, as Omar-Jo had
been. He worshiped Charlot, whose name was linked with

misfortunes, but who knew how to distract others with his troubles. To distract himself.

"You really think it's a good idea?"

The whole situation seemed incongruous to him. In addition, those three unrelated names—from different countries, even different continents—were sign of a cosmopolitan point of view that had nothing good about it.

"It's a very good idea. It'll make you a lot of money."

The child had inherited a sharp business sense from his ancestors—navigators, champions of commerce, they'd set up trading posts around the perimeter of the Mediterranean since antiquity.

"You'll see, I'll bring you crowds. I'll make them laugh. I'll make them laugh . . . laugh till they cry."

He stumbled over the last word. "Cry" evoked too much blood spilled, too many real tragedies, too much real-life anguish.

Hastily, he caught himself. "I meant 'double up with laughter.' They'll double up with laughter. You'll see."

OMAR-JO CAME BACK day after day. It was vacation; he had lots of free time.

"We'll put posters around the square. I'll make them myself, with my three names."

The child's words had concrete results; he always found a way to put his ideas into effect. Carried along by the current, Maxime let things happen. They agreed on lots of points: they decided to keep longer hours; they bought Chinese lanterns, which formed a glittering crown around the cupola.

The prizes—lollipops and various sweets—had reappeared. Omar-Jo appeared among the children in various disguises to guide them to their places, set them on their mounts, tie them on. A greater and greater number of boys and girls hurried there; the boy was counting on his future show to bring in many more.

After the children disappeared, a few nostalgic adults couldn't resist the pleasure of taking a turn. One evening, even Maxime was surprised to find himself astride the cherry bay while Omar-Jo beat time to the music as he walked around the carousel.

"AND YOUR FAMILY? You told me you had a family here."

"They're cousins: Rosie and Antoine. They have a laundry."

"What do they think of all this?"

"They let me do what I want. I'm on vacation."

"Well, *I* want everything to be done right. I don't want any problems."

"I'll ask them to come to see you."

Tormented by her married life, which was scarcely going along as she had expected—there was no sign of a break with Claudette—Rosie decided to change her appearance again, to revive her dying coquetry. She gave up her chignon, dyed her white strands of hair. She revealed her shapely legs and impudent breasts again, by wearing less enveloping skirts, tighter blouses. In a short time, she seduced a young bookseller who brought in his laundry to be washed by the pound every Tuesday.

Both Antoine and Rosie, absorbed in their business

affairs, were relieved to learn that "that unhappy child trau-
matized by the war" had just found an amusing job, which
would perhaps become lucrative. Omar-Jo had persuaded
them that after the apprenticeship, the *forain* would pay
him for his services. During the school year, he would continue to devote a few hours a week to the Merry-go-round,
as well as Sundays and holidays.

One afternoon, the cousins decided to go there to make
Maxime's acquaintance. The couple and Maxime congratulated each other:
  "Your little cousin is a go-getter."
  "It's true your Merry-go-round is really beautiful."
  He found them reassuring, proper. Trying to reassure
them, he, in turn, promised to guarantee the child all his
meals when he was there with him. They left each other on
the best of terms.
  . Every evening, Omar-Jo and Maxime left in opposite
directions to go to their respective homes. Sometimes,
evenings lasting longer, the child got permission to sleep at
the *forain*'s. He'd arranged a spot to sleep on the divan in
the second room.

Every year in August, Antoine and Rosie went back to their cottage near Port-Miou.

He devoted himself to the pleasure of fishing. She would take a little dip, then go home to do the cleaning and cooking; she scaled and cleaned the fish her husband brought back until she was nauseated.

The child had asked to stay in Paris.

"There are lots of plans for the Merry-go-round. Maxime needs me. I can't leave."

Rosie had agreed immediately. Since Claudette had gone off, Rosie's countless intimate talks with Antoine would help bring them closer together.

Such was not the case. Always avoiding the heart of the matter, they recalled their childhood; their common past; their little, agonized country. They squabbled about everything, each taking a different side. They got to the point of quarreling about the child. There, too, they differed in their points of view, or, rather, their views changed constantly: one always took the opposite position, whatever it might be, to that of the other spouse.

"My poor cousin Annette. It would have been better for everyone if she'd married someone of her own religion," sighed Rosie.

"What's the good of regrets? What good does it do?"

"Annette did everything wrong."

"Don't condemn Annette."

"What was she thinking of when she made Omar leave Egypt?"

"That's news to me; it's the first time I've heard she made him do anything at all! They both agreed on the marriage."

"What does he do? I can't remember now."

"A driver. A chauffeur."

"Starting as a general maid, Annette became a 'young female companion.' She could have married someone with a better job, more enterprising . . . someone like you, Antoine."

Sometimes, in desperation, Rosie tried to flatter her husband to win his favors.

"Thanks to you, Antoine. Look how far we've come."

He returned the compliment. "You had something to do with it too, Rosie."

"It's the man who gives strength to the couple."

"A couple is the man *and* the woman," he replied.

She stared at him, dumbfounded. In just a few months, had Claudette been able to root out prejudices to which Rosie had always yielded?

"Life didn't give Annette and Omar time to prove what they could do," continued Antoine.

"Annette wasn't ugly. Do you remember? Too skinny maybe."

"I don't think so."

"Her hair was so straight, her nose a little long, she had very pale skin. And she was timid, so very timid."

"She was just sweet, that's all. That was her charm."

"Hmmm. You think so? . . . it's true that Cousin Robert, the one who made his fortune in Brazil, would have been glad to marry her. She thought he was too old, and too rich. Can you imagine, 'too rich'!?"

"I like Omar-Jo," cut in Antoine. "He's quick, resourceful. He could have done a bunch of things for us. Now it's too late. He's started out at the Merry-go-round."

"Perhaps it isn't too late."

After reflecting a few minutes, she continued, "This winter, shall we take him to Sunday mass? We don't even know what his religion is. Did old Joseph say anything about it on the telephone?"

"We'll ask the child; he's forthright. As for old Joseph, he used to speak to God face-to-face. He didn't need intermediaries, he said. I don't think he's changed."

"An old pagan, right. Yet, he's the one they always sent for to lead the procession at all the ceremonies."

Illiterate, signing only with an ink-smudged thumb, old Joseph was the best storyteller of the region. During get-togethers on a winter evening, those who lived nearby gathered around him. On long summer evenings, other villagers crossed the hills to hear him.

He also excelled at singing and dancing. They called on him for baptisms, marriages, burials. Dressed all in white or in black, depending on the circumstances, it was he who preceded and led the procession.

He was husky and bore his five feet seven inches so proudly that he seemed ten inches taller. A slightly hooked nose, full lips, his gray eyes—sometimes grave, sometimes laughing—gave his face an air of nobility and goodness.

Depending on whether it was a celebration or mourning, he either raised the two ends of his mustache and stuck them in position, or let them droop at each side of his mouth. His black, curly mop of hair, salt and pepper as he aged, covered the nape of his neck.

Old Joseph's voice was resonant; his handshake, warm.

He didn't fear the cold, the heat, dryness or humidity, neither snow nor rain; and in all kinds of weather, he wore a collarless shirt, which left his powerful neck free, and which was left open enough to reveal his hairy chest. He would thump it with his bent index finger:

"Concrete. It's like concrete. But inside, a bird sings and beats its wings."

Leading the processions, Joseph swung a large, curved saber with a silver pommel in circles over his head. It was his most precious possession.

He wore very loose trousers, tight around the ankles. Rising on one foot, he would pirouette in one direction, then in the other; he turned like a top before he came to the final pause, which let him calmly regain his balance.

After this introduction, his song rose up, a mixture of ritual prayers and improvised words. His warm, unparalleled voice opened hearts, a remedy for sorrows.

"If you weren't so bawdy or less of an unbeliever . . . ," scolded the priest, endowed, as many mountain priests are, with a swarm of children, "I would have entrusted you with the mission of calling the faithful to services from the bell tower." He appreciated this custom of the other religion's initiates a great deal. "But I know you. You're likely to invent your own words . . . and then where would we be?"

Widower of a spouse whom he had cherished tenderly, alone, Joseph had raised his only daughter, Annette. When his wife, Adele, died, he was fifty; his sexual appetites had not died.

Every two weeks, he entrusted his little girl to neighbors

and disappeared. He was supposed to go to the city, he would say, to finish up urgent business. They pretended to believe him! It was widely known that he was unlike his compatriots in his singular inaptitude for business. Whether it was a transaction involving an inherited piece of land or the sale of products from his garden, his dealings always turned out disastrously. "I don't like money enough," he would say as an excuse.

Living on little, with pleasure, he considered wealth and the desire some had for it a rein to his freedom or, at least, the feeling he had about his freedom.

Staying with prostitutes in town—one or the other of them, he didn't care which—he visited them free of charge. He did them small favors, brightened up their evenings with dances, songs, and stories. They always welcomed him with open arms.

A large number of them came from central Europe, from the Baltic states, for their blondness was especially appreciated here. Others arrived from Latin America, France, Spain, Italy. Joseph asked them questions; he visited the world by listening to them.

To him the world seemed vast, marvelous, hybrid, teeming. On all sides, loves and violence, faithfulness and betrayal, injustices and liberty suddenly sprang forth. The same dreams, the same despairs, the same rebirths. And everywhere, the same death. A tenacious solidarity should bind all human beings together, it seemed to him, when they saw the basic, self-evident image of death.

"No need to leave my little corner of the earth. Beautiful

Women, I embark on your bodies. I go all over the world on your words." He wished real trips for other people and for the child of his only child too.

Since Adele's death, he avoided meeting Nawal, a prostitute who'd been the wife of his neighbor, a peddler. He had loved her long ago, desired her madly; his silent wife had probably suffered because of it. Joseph erased the memory of his offense by making an extra effort to care for Adele's daughter, Annette, and to show her tenderness.

Annette had a happy childhood. Later, Joseph approved of her marriage to Omar, the young man of a different religion whom Joseph adopted at first sight. He was able to convince his village that the marriage should be approved. It welcomed the young man and later was sorry to see him leave for the capital with his wife, shortly after the birth of little Omar-Jo.

The child was born at the time when the first hostilities were breaking out. In spite of the upheavals, people were convinced that they were only temporary tremors. Between brothers, the worst strife cannot go on forever.

The struggles went on forever. Often joined with, fed, reinforced by the outside world. More than ten years had passed.

Old Joseph, who'd just reached eighty, learned, in the middle of the afternoon, that a car armed with explosives had just blown up in the neighborhood where Annette lived. He had been listening to the transistor radio hanging around his neck while he worked in the garden.

He tried to leave his hill as soon as possible to go down to the capital. Panting, distraught, he knocked at the doors of neighbors with vehicles. Most of them weren't home; others were hesitant to take the plunge into hell.

"Why imagine the worst? Things have been breaking down, smashing to bits everywhere for years. Nothing has happened to your family. Nothing will happen to them."

"I want to be sure."

Not far away, young Edouard was repairing his motorcycle.

"I'll take you where you want."

He climbed on his machine, pumped the pedal, pivoted

the handlebars, gunned the motor while the old man took a place on the rear seat.

"Go on, as fast as you can. I'll show you the shortcuts."

He knew his mountain by heart, from its splendrous summits to its smallest escarpments. The muffler made such a racket that the old man put his lips close to the young man's temple to whisper the right directions in his ear. The roads were badly paved, bumpy; they hoped that the machine—secondhand, rather worn out—would hold up. They also counted on escaping the various armed groups, of all sides or of no side, who stopped vehicles to check them or to ask for a bribe.

Once at the exact spot of the catastrophe, they could approach only on foot.

The authorities had just isolated the exploded car. Around the site, a large area was marked off by red stakes stuck in the ground and tied together by a rope. The detonation had taken place at the very foot of his children's building. Joseph felt his knees give way; his heart was in his throat.

He forced his way between the police and the screaming crowd, slipped under the security rope, followed by Edouard.

Suddenly, facing the monstrous carcass, he felt a surge of denial and decided to climb to the apartment, convinced that there he would find Omar, Annette, and Omar-Jo.

His strength came back, like lightning. Shooting up from his heels, it straightened his legs, raised, lifted his old body, propelling him to attack the hundred steps. With the young man at his heels, he reached the sixth floor quickly.

The door of the home was still ajar.   57

He called. Inside, he searched everywhere. It didn't take long. He found no one.

In the living room, he almost slipped on some colored pencils scattered over the flagstones and nearly sprawled out full length.

He went out on the balcony. Nobody there either.

Gasping for breath, he went back down to join the multitude crowded around the destroyed automobile. Blinded by the curtains of yellow dust, Joseph walked with his arms stretched out before him to avoid obstacles. Catching the ambulance driver by the arm, he asked for the victims' names and the list of hospitals. He got no answer.

"I know the hospitals. We'll go around to them together," Edouard suggested. "If they're hurt, they'll be fixed up there."

The old man was trying to convince himself that his little family had been out of the neighborhood at the time of the explosion. However — up there! — that open door undermined his confidence. He went forward, his eyes to the ground as he looked for traces of them, hoping he would find none.

He did.

First: a scrap of the orange-flowered dress. Next: Omar's unusual ring, set with a sand-colored scarab. This time, gathering up things, he was certain of their disappearance.

"What did you find?" asked the young man.

He held back from saying, "They are dead," as if once

those words were pronounced, Omar and Annette were irremediably condemned; the words would destroy the last illusion to which Joseph still clung in spite of the evidence.

Moving like a robot, he continued his search. He moved aside the debris, combed the crevices with a stick. After a quarter of an hour, he discovered one of Omar-Jo's sandals on the edge of a pit. He could have picked it out from a thousand others! He was the one who had replaced the worn strap with this one, thicker and crudely sewn.

Farther away, a few feet from the deadly mechanism— the wrecked car looked like a hydra about to be reborn, spring up, level everything—the old man was again confronted with horror.

He had just recognized the arm of his grandson sticking out of a piece of a blue T-shirt.

His stick fell from his hands. His powerful frame reeled, shrank up inside him until he seemed a clump of dirt. Burning lead poured into his bowels.

Edouard approached cautiously. Sensing catastrophe, he touched the old man's shoulder as a sign that he was there with him, attentive. Then the young man leaned down to kiss Joseph between the shoulder blades.

"I'm here. I'm not leaving you."

Then, he waited.

Immobile for a long while, Joseph set off once again. A tragic rage galvanized him. His feet hammered the ground, the storm set his features ablaze.

He sprinted up the closest heap of rubble and debris. Planted on the summit of the mound, he lifted his arms to the sky. A sky of periwinkle blue. The succession of fires flaring, the rising ashes could not dull its celestial brightness. That sky! For a few moments, he cursed it. That impenetrable sky, its secrets locked away!

"I will never sing again! I shall never dance again! For what, for whom, those celebrations, those ceremonies! Never again!" he howled.

Was he addressing someone? That God who was of no concern to him, and who suddenly imposed his presence upon him by this disaster, these questions, his own maledictions? His brother Job—the one in the Bible of his youth —with his provocative, rebellious words, came back to mind. Would he be at peace again in the end, as Job had been? Would he be reconciled, later, with that savage God who became a lamb?

Right now, he raged, turning his fury against men. The men of this city, those in nearby lands, all the men in the universe.

"Criminals! Fratricides! Killers of innocents! You will never stop killing and hating each other! Where does all that bring you? Into the grave a little faster. Into the same enormous grave!"

As he looked down at the chaotic amphitheater of stones, scrap iron, bones, of flesh and of blood, the imposing silhouette of the old man riveted to his mound filled the horizon. Surrounded by curtains of yellowish sand, his form, fleshy and ghostly, appeared, disappeared from the sight of the crowd.

Holding back his tears, which would have bowed him down and shaken him with sobs, Joseph rose up on his toes and stretched out all his muscles, tensing them until they ached.

TWO ARMS had just come around his hips. Someone was trying to pull him, to make him come down from his butte. A woman's cry cut through the din:

"Your grandson is alive! I saw the ambulance drivers carry Omar-Jo away."

Joseph stiffened, freed himself roughly from the hold. He had just recognized Nawal's voice.

"No more lies. You always lie! Go! Get away!"

Increasing her efforts, she finally dislodged him from the mound. Bringing him to her, Nawal drew him to her breast, then rocked him like a child.

"Believe me, I saw Omar-Jo leaving on his own two feet. With my own eyes. I saw him."

It was true. She recognized the child of this child, the child of Annette, who could have been her own. Leaning out of her window a little after the explosion, she had seen the boy struggling to get away from the ambulance drivers in spite of his blood-soaked shoulder. He stubbornly insisted upon staying to find his mother and father.

Nawal's ears were still ringing with their two names, which he cried out endlessly in his heartbreaking voice.

But it had been too late for Omar-Jo. His parents had been blown up by the fatal bomb. Later blasts and fragments of metal wounded other residents of the quarter very seriously and tore away his left arm.

Nawal had seen everything. She could testify to each

moment of the scene. She affirmed that the child, who had
lost great quantities of blood, had finally yielded to the
ambulance drivers and let himself be taken away.

"You must believe me: Omar-Jo is alive."

For a few seconds, the sensual perfume of incense and
jasmine, the timbre of that incandescent voice, the burning
breath on his neck, the nearness of the familiar body, blot-
ted out the time and place of the calamity. For only a few
seconds—in spite of the many years gone by—they rekin-
dled a strange fever. Old Joseph closed his eyelids; a shiver
of pleasure ran down his spine.

Then, annoyed with himself, he immediately regained
his self-control.

"Liar! Don't keep on lying."

She relaxed her embrace, then glanced at him sorrow-
fully before turning her back and hobbling away.

"Old fool," she grumbled tenderly. "You'll never
change."

He watched her leave; she would vanish, come back
into sight, disappear again, limping slightly, in the midst of
veils of dust.

Under her skinny body, under her white, bristling hair,
under the stumbling walk, there was still the same Nawal he
had so wildly possessed.

"You've always lied," he heard himself repeating, filled
with a flood of memories.

Joseph, who hated lies, had begun to lie. To lie to Elias, a peddler, his best friend, whose wife was Nawal. To lie to Adele, his wife, soon to be pregnant with Annette.

They had made love. Anywhere; anytime. Below the spring, under the olive tree, among the pines, on the burning stones of the terrace, in the conjugal bed. Nawal would manage to get word to Joseph, who lived in a neighboring village, as soon as Elias left on his rounds.

Their time was limited; she would rush to him, naked under her dress. The thirst to be united tormented them. They took each other, took each other again, over and over. They intoxicated each other with caresses and kisses.

"Cure me of you, Nawal," he begged.

She would repeat, "Cure me of you."

Adele kept silent. Had she suspected their relationship? He didn't try to find out. He avoided his wife's eyes and stayed away from his friend. They had tried to leave each

other several times. But it was impossible to break their ties,   63
binding in pleasure as in grief.

Adele passed away giving birth to Annette.

Consumed with remorse, Joseph was finally able to
break with Nawal. The young woman, respectful of the
dead woman's memory, disappeared.

She left the village, never to appear there again. Her
husband's, Elias's, efforts to find her were fruitless. He
became resigned to his loss and died, run over by a truck,
in the course of his wanderings.

During one of the nights when Joseph took refuge at the
prostitutes', he went upstairs to a room with one of them.

Suddenly, the door opened, the lights went out. A
woman entered. By mutual agreement, she replaced the
first. The act of love took on a different savor.

As soon as he recognized Nawal, she slipped out of
sight. This time, forever.

Later, Joseph was to learn that Nawal had a child by a sailor
whose ship had spent a month in dock.

Long years afterward, she helped her son get a start in
life; she provided the financing and helped with the organi-
zation of his paint business. She also took care of deliveries,
driving the truck herself to different corners of the country.

Since Adele's death, Joseph had devoted himself to his
daughter. Annette had inherited patience and candor from
her mother. He tried to protect her from all danger, espe-

64   cially from men of his sort, whose hot blood and impetu-
ousness would have made her suffer.

When Annette presented Omar to him, he consented
immediately. He had sized up the young man in the blink
of an eye. Omar was both healthy and gentle, merry and
calm. He would make his daughter happy; Joseph was sure
of that.

Joseph found his grandson at the hospital. He had to wait several weeks before he could bring him home.

The same night as the accident, the old man, accompanied by Edouard, had gone back to the disaster site to try to save Omar's and Annette's remains from the common grave. They evaded roadblocks, crossed through the mob.

Joseph piled everything that had belonged to them in an empty toolbox, which Edouard held open by its double handles: pieces of the material of the flowered dress, rags of the beige checked shirt, of blue jeans; a part of Annette's shopping bag, one of the compartments of his son-in-law's wallet. Scraps of flesh stuck to the fragments.

Later, always with Edouard, the old man went to the cemetery of his community.

Asma, the caretaker of the graves, an eccentric and tyrannical woman, was wandering along the cemetery paths, as she usually did, in search of her husband.

He, so she said, stuffed himself with food, deprived his children of theirs. Then, to digest what he'd eaten and to sleep in peace the rest of the day, he took shelter in a prominent citizen's burial vault. Spacious, provided with a funerary chapel, cooler in summer, warmer in winter, those mausoleums had all the advantages. They also allowed him to escape his wife and the irksome chores she tried to impose on him.

He changed mausoleums constantly, so Asma couldn't track him down. Now, giving up her unseemly and useless forays, most of the time she merely shrieked out across the cemetery, summoning the angels, the saints, the dead of high rank to her rescue; calling as well to her brood of children who also fled before her. "Your lazy, rotten father is eating your bread, my poor little children! And you, respectable dead, he's made you accomplices to his evil deeds!"

Edouard and old Joseph caught sight of the caretaker from a distance. She was, as usual, fulminating. Her red, shaggy hair, her bellicose visage stood out above the turbulent billows of her vast black robes, which came down to her ankles.

The cemeteries were strictly separated according to religion, and even according to the different rituals within a religion—this little country counted about fifteen, differing only in minor ways.

Determined not to begin a discussion with Asma, whose superficial religiosity took offense at any mixture of doctrines or liturgies, old Joseph had decided—it was an

unspoken promise to them—not to separate in death those
two beings so perfectly joined in life.

He held out a considerable sum of money to the caretaker before making his request. Unable to resist the money
she saw, she stuffed the bills into her pocket with a false bottom, the one she'd fashioned in secret, in hiding from her
worthless spouse.

The old man showed her the box Edouard was carrying.
He asked for a modest site for his children. He had spotted
a corner below the crumbling outside wall of the cemetery,
which looked out on fields, then out on the sea in the distance.

"Who are they?" asked the caretaker.

"The explosion of the car bomb . . . killed on the spot.
My daughter, her husband."

"That's all that's left of those children of God?"

"That's all."

"Was your son-in-law of the same sect as you?" she
questioned with a knowing air, never suspecting that he was
of a different belief.

"A child of God," muttered the old man.

That satisfied her.

"That's what we're doing to all of the children of God,"
she moaned, as she fingered the money in her pocket with
satisfaction.

With Edouard's help, Joseph buried the box. He rolled a
scrap of the orange-flowered material around a stake
instead of a wreath, and planted it in the ground. He found
a piece of white marble on a ruined grave, took it over to

68   the burial plot. Placing it on the small square of ground,
with his multiple-blade pocketknife, he patiently carved
upon it the two entwined initials "A&O."

As soon as Omar-Jo was well, he would point out the tomb
to him. Later, he would slip Omar's ring, with its sacred
scarab, on his grandson's finger.

What a clown!" exclaimed Maxime with a laugh.

Each day for the last two weeks, Omar-Jo had invented a new accoutrement. This time, it was wings; they grew out of him everywhere. Paper wings, cloth wings, plastic wings —all painted in gaudy colors with grotesque faces that floated like water lilies among flamboyant geometric designs. On his giant, red nose perched an immense wasp. Instead of eyebrows, the musical symbol for a flat note was drawn upside down.

He'd persuaded Antoine and Rosie to give him a cheap harmonica, from which he extracted many strange vibrations; sometimes, he added a farcical tremolo or a strident squawk that drew all eyes toward him.

Informed by word of mouth and by posters put about the Place, the public was beginning to flood in.

"I know what's coming," grumbled Maxime. "Soon you'll be asking for a salary."

"Give me a ride in your coach from time to time, keep

on feeding me, and I'll give you all the rest for free. 'Gratis,' as I've said before."

"Gratis is okay with me."

The adventure had given Maxime an appetite. He would rub his hands together when he saw the lengthening line of little boys and girls waiting impatiently to storm the Merry-go-round. Certain adults are sorry they've outgrown the body they wore as a child, that free body, that light body, which once turned to the music on the steeds of their fantasies.

In the evening, when Maxime and the child together covered the bright figures with the dark tarp, they felt the same sadness, the same feeling of an inevitable separation.

"We'll have to think about a night show," suggested the child.

"Night show? Aren't you getting me in too deep?"

Omar-Jo had already persuaded the *forain* to start the game with the rings again and the handing out of lollipops that followed. Sometimes, he added a photomaton print of his face made up in different disguises; or else his stump would be transformed into a fountain from which artificial flowers or many-colored ribbons cascaded.

You only have to sow certain words to reap a harvest. The words "night shows" would come to Maxime's mind more and more often, the child was sure. All he had to do was wait; Omar-Jo could be patient.

BEFORE SHE LEFT for Port-Miou, Rosie had been concerned about her young nephew, whom she'd left with Maxime. Yet, the man had made a good impression on them. Antoine reassured her completely. The child would adapt even quicker that way; his entire nature seemed to push him toward other people.

"Do you think he's eating right?" she worried.

Because food is one of the strongest ties many emigrants have with their ancestral past, Rosie wondered if Omar-Jo hadn't missed the dishes of his country during their absence. When she asked Omar-Jo about it, he was surprised; he liked those dishes more than others, but with his adventurous nature, he was not inclined to nostalgia. He missed only the people he loved, sometimes to the point of torment.

"I've got an idea," proposed Rosie. "I'll cook one of our specialties just for Maxime. You'll take it to him for me. You can share it then."

"I'm not sure he'll like it."

"People always like our food," she declared.

She concocted a meat pie mixed with cracked wheat, which she filled with chopped beef, fried onions, pine nuts; and a puree of chick peas sprinkled with olive oil to go with it.

"You'll see, he'll be pleased."

Omar-Jo doubted it.

PRECEDED by the strong odor of food, he appeared before the *forain,* holding the platter covered with aluminum foil in his only arm.

"What're you hiding under that?"

"One of our native dishes. It's for you, from my cousin."

With his fingertips, Maxime raised the foil.

"It's swimming in oil and grease. Disastrous for my arteries! Get it out of here!"

Expecting this reception, the child retraced his steps without a word. On the way, he wondered how to give the food back to Rosie, without seriously offending her.

Suddenly, he thought of the vagrant he came across on his way every morning.

She sat, her back against a wall, at the corner of the Grands Magasins. Wearing three woolen caps of different colors, one over the other, short boots of greenish rubber on her feet, she was surrounded by a protective fence of a half-dozen blue plastic sacks, filled to overflowing. With what she collected every dawn from garbage cans in the vicinity, her miserable possessions grew from day to day. She had no known address. She was part of the decor; nobody thought of asking her to clear out.

Omar-Jo was fascinated by the theatrical aspect of this personage, and he felt an extreme pity for her face, still young but horribly puffy, for her swollen, mauve lips, her dirty neck, her battered fingers, which stuck out of filthy mittens. She must have endured many misfortunes to come to this point. As for misfortunes, he knew.

The homeless woman felt drawn to the one-armed boy with the hollow in his cheek. In their mutual sympathy, they expected nothing of each other but this connivance, this silent complicity. Neither of them ever asked any questions.

Each morning, as he passed by, the child greeted her. "Have a good day, madame."

She answered playfully, "Have a good day, monsieur."

When Omar-Jo presented the food to her, the homeless

woman clapped her hands. Immediately, she pulled a worn-out basin out of one of her sacks and asked him to pour the food into it.

"That smells really good. What a treat!"

She scraped out the bottom of the dish with her bread. He was happy, relieved. This evening when he went home, he could tell Rosie that Maxime had appreciated her cooking so much that there was nothing left. "Look, not a single crumb," he would insist.

Before leaving, he slipped a few words into the bag lady's ear: "One day, you'll be invited to the Merry-go-round."

"I'll come!" she replied.

He could imagine her, a witch or a fairy, suddenly emerging from the coach to dance and sing on the turning platform.

Omar-Jo arrived at the Merry-go-round at the noon break. He found a note from Maxime fastened to the window of the booth; it asked him to meet him at a neighboring bistro.

He found the *forain* before a bottle of Beaujolais, digging into a copious dish of sausages and fries.

"Come and eat, kid!"

"And your arteries?" laughed Omar-Jo. "All of a sudden, you don't think about them anymore."

Omar-Jo accompanied the cavalcade in a hundred ways: standing on one of the wooden horses or leaping from the coach like a jack-in-the-box, he went, came, danced, gave his spiel, often spoke directly to the spectators.

Girls and boys hurried there in ever-greater numbers.

Bewitched by the spectacle, the parents paid without complaint. Business continued to prosper. Maxime bought the latest popular records; he lit the lanterns earlier and earlier.

The Merry-go-round owner again declined the Sunday invitations of his family. They were disappointed to learn that he was no longer going to get rid of the carousel. On the contrary, he was getting to like it again, and he devoted most of his time to it.

"How are you going to get by? You were telling us yourself . . ."

"Right now, I'm getting along, I'm even managing very well."

They couldn't understand it at all. His voice was jovial, gay. Perhaps he'd been drinking? When you live alone like that! . . . They thought of sending a scout to the capital, someone close to him who could reason with him. They consulted each other without coming to an agreement.

When he felt his public with him, applauding and laughing at his craziness, Omar-Jo changed his repertoire abruptly.

First, he turned off the music, his buffoonery shattering against an invisible wall. Then, he let a deep silence hover over the spectators.

With one motion, he tore out the ribbons or greenery that hid his stump. Then, he presented the stump to the public in all its brutal reality.

He took off his false nose. Rubbing his face with the tail of his shirt, he cleaned off his makeup. His ashen face appeared; his sunken eyes were an infinite black.

He had also shed his disguises, which lay in a pile at his feet. He stamped on them, then climbing on the mound of their remains, he began to speak again.

They were other words.

They rose from his depths, tearing Omar-Jo away from the atmosphere that he himself had created. Forgetting his tricks, he let that voice rise within him. That harsh voice, that bare voice, covered all the other voices.

The multiple child was no longer there to entertain. He was there to evoke images. All those painful images that fill the world.

Led by his voice, Omar-Jo evokes his city, left so recently. It seeps into his muscles, filters into his heartbeat, slows the journey of his blood. He sees it, he touches it, his faraway city. He compares it to this one, where you may freely go, come, breathe. This one already his, which he already loves so tenderly.

Here, trees escort the avenues, surround the squares. Solid buildings revive forgotten centuries; others foretell the future. A diverse population strolls or hastens on. In spite of problems and cares, they live in peace. In peace!

There, pockets of ruin multiply, uprooted trees rot at the bottom of fissures, walls are riddled with bullets, cars explode, buildings collapse. From one side to the other of a city that's smashed to bits, human beings are liquidated at a cheap price.

Omar-Jo unleashes his fury; his words are ablaze. Omar-Jo is no longer playing. He contemplates the world and what he already knows of it. His appeals grow louder; he's not only speaking for his own. All the miseries of the world stampede toward the Merry-go-round.

Everything has come to a stop. The horses have ended their round. The public listens, petrified.

Maxime, confused, doesn't dare silence the strange child.

After those cries of anguish, the only solution is to take up
life again.

Omar-Jo pulls his old harmonica out of his pocket again, and getting his breath back, he draws melodic, lively music from it one more time.

Slowly, the Merry-go-round begins to turn again.

No longer sure if it has just plunged into the cruelest reality or if it has only witnessed a pantomime, the crowd applauds.

"Where did you get all those things at your age?" asked Maxime later in the evening.

"One day, I'll tell you."

"Sometimes you speak like a child, sometimes like an adult. When are you yourself, Omar-Jo?"

"Each time."

THE PROPRIETOR was determined to ask the child about his past. He questioned him again the very next day.

"Your arm? What exactly happened to it?"

"Drop it."

"An accident?"

"An accident. What do you want me to say?"

"*I* don't want anything. I just want to know, that's all. What kind of accident?"

"The war . . ."

"One more of those barbaric wars!"

"No more barbaric than any other, " the child retorted.

"I wasn't attacking you."

Because of their mixed marriage, Omar and Annette had been more interested than some in history. There had always been books in Omar-Jo's house. Since the beginning of humanity, barbarism had drenched the world with blood; in Europe, only a short time ago, horror had reigned everywhere.

"I didn't mean to attack you," repeated Maxime. "Does all that have something to do with religion? In what God do you believe?"

"There is only one God," replied the child, "even if the paths aren't the same. My mother and father knew it. They died in the same acts of violence, in the same explosion. If I do believe, it's in one God. But people don't want to see. They are blind."

Maxime wondered if he had faith himself. If he did, what kind? He took part in religious ceremonies that every time became the occasion for parties and abundant feasts; outside of that, he hardly practiced his religion.

Trying to continue the dialogue with the child, he went on: "Do you know that certain crusaders left from this Place, right here where we are, to go to your lands?"

"I know. Wars flourished in those times too."

"They fought, but sometimes they came to terms too. I gathered information about all that. Saladin was always ready to take the peaceful way. In one period, a true entente had been arranged between Christians and Muslims. Frederick I, the Germanic emperor, wrote to the sultan of Cairo, 'I am your friend.' Did you know that a certain Nicholas Flamel was close to men on the other side of the Mediterranean."

"I know," said the child. "It was like you and me."

"Why not? And maybe we'll find the philosophers' stone, the one that changes everything into gold."

"We'll change everything into gold," said the child. "You'll see."

"Your arm, Omar-Jo? You still haven't told me how you lost it."

Omar-Jo hadn't felt it when his arm was torn away nor the impact of the metal fragment going through his cheek. The disappearance of Omar and Annette had made him insensitive to any other pain.

Several hours afterward, the child awoke in a hospital bed. Only then did he remember the killing field, emerging from clouds of sticky, yellow dust. Again, he saw the heaps of cement blocks and scrap metal, the gaping belly of the bombed-out car; the entanglement of pistons, connecting rods, windows, fenders, and wheels made it look like a monstrous beast, greedy for human sacrifice.

Omar-Jo looked for his arm, then his left hand. He looked for the arm he'd held before him, for the hand that had pushed aside the rubble to pick up a piece of material with orange flowerlets.

But he didn't find them.

SOON OLD JOSEPH took his grandson home with him to the mountain.

After a month—hostilities having been interrupted once more—he confided to him that he'd buried his parents' remains in the square plot of ground.

Omar-Jo wanted to go there alone. The old man wasn't opposed to it. He and his grandson were alike: their decision made, nobody could sway them.

The cemetery, located in a suburb close to combat zones, had had its share of projectiles. It looked devastated.

Enclosed by a partially fallen wall, the vaults had a border of anemic Judas trees, puny shrubs, and molting palms around them. The grill of the main entrance lay on the ground among bumps and holes. Farther away, some gravestones, gray, split, had been hastily replaced by a series of wobbly bricks held together by a layer of black cement. A tipcart containing shovels, spades, files, and the cart's wheel lay on its side.

Everything attested to the negligence of the groundskeeper. Sheltered in a mausoleum, he, as usual, was dozing peacefully.

Omar-Jo went along the main path in the middle of a dozen mausoleums, some of which had funerary chapels. Their sumptuous appearance, damaged through twelve years of spasmodic bombing, was supposed to guarantee their occupants the same status in the next world as the status they'd enjoyed in this one.

The groundskeeper was pleased the notables' families were absent, most of them gone abroad. That way he could make use of their tombs, as he wished.

As soon as Omar-Jo appeared, a mastiff without a collar

came out of his kennel, approached, growling and showing his fangs. Hiding his fear, the child went on his way. As did the animal.

They met again face-to-face. The growls had changed into barks, which alerted Asma at the other end of the cemetery. She rushed toward them, shouting. The sound of her voice was enough; the animal was rooted to the spot, his legs stiff.

A tornado suddenly loomed up at the end of the path; green babouches slapped the grave keeper's heels; her black robes seethed, swollen with fury. Her head was crowned with a mop of reddish hair, wild, henna dyed. Brought up short by this sudden apparition, by the quivering head of hair, which seemed to be swarming with little snakes, the child was taken aback.

Asma had hurried in hopes of finding a repentant owner at the end of her run. Suddenly taken with remorse upon his return to the country, the owner was probably coming to reward her for the care she'd lavished upon his dear departed. The sight of the child surprised and disappointed her. Approaching, she noticed his patched cheek and his amputation. He was probably coming to beg. Why did she —she, poverty stricken herself—have to help others even more destitute?

"Alms? . . . I'm not a beggar. I'm the grandson of Joseph H. It's my grandfather who sent me. A month ago, he buried my mother and father in this cemetery."

She remembered. The old man had paid her handsomely for the tiny piece of ground. Thinking that Joseph had charged the boy to pay her again, she graced him with a radiant smile.

"Your grandfather was a prince. A real prince. The descendant of the prince is welcome!"

She bent down, placed her two palms on each side of the dog's rump and pushed the dog forward with all her might.

"Out of sight, brute! This boy is like a son to me. Go lie down, Lotus. Lie down, I said!"

His tail between his legs, the mastiff didn't need to be told again. Slowly, he went toward his second refuge, dug in the shade of an ancient funerary stela. The compost, recently turned over, would provide a comfortable coolness in the next few hours, which promised to be torrid.

"Did your grandfather give you a message for me?"

"He told me: 'Asma will keep her word; she'll show you the location!'"

"Nothing else?"

"Nothing else."

Nothing but deceits! Hiding her disappointment, she tried to make up for it at the same time: "First, you must do something for me."

"If you want," said the child.

Immediately, wanting to exonerate herself with Joseph, whom the boy would inevitably tell about the visit, she called upon the boy to bear witness to her miseries by launching into one of her habitual diatribes.

"You will repeat to your grandfather that I'm married to a good-for-nothing, to a parasite! All he thinks about is eating, taking naps. He even goes so far as to desecrate the inside of the burial vaults by . . ."

She stopped short; she sighed, sniffled before starting out again.

"No, I can't repeat that. You're only a child, after all. But Joseph will understand! Tell him that I must be silent about some things because you're so young! Do you understand? . . . you will add that that lazy bum changes his hiding place, so that I'll lose his trail. He's made his own children accomplices in this abominable game. For weeks, he hasn't even come home to sleep at night. It's a good thing Lotus is here to defend us, me and my children. In these terrible times, there are thieves, marauders, assassins everywhere."

Her hands cupped around her mouth, Asma began to call her horde of kids in a thundering voice.

"Saïd! Elias! Where are you hiding, sons of a dog! There's work to be done over here! . . . Marie! Emma! Soad! You have hearts of stone, not the hearts of daughters! . . . Naguib! Brahim! Boutras! Where are you, my children? You will all bring me to my death!"

She threatened to tear her breast, scratch her face bloody. She gestured wildly. Raising her tragedienne's sleeves, she shook her flowing, swirling robes.

Considering this excessiveness with an understanding and indulgent eye, taking her fatigue, her exasperation, and her outrageous character into account, the child remained calm, waiting for the storm to clear.

The caretaker's voice subsided.

Her robes gathered around her, her hair smoothed, she leaned on the boy's shoulder and murmured plaintively, "It's true they'll be the death of me. All the work—I do it all alone, after all I'm only a woman! You tell your grandfather. You will tell him that's the reason I asked you to help me out. Just an hour or two. Then, I'll show you your parents' grave."

She stooped down, kissed him on the forehead.

"The war really fixed you up, poor little fellow."

"I'll help you," he said, in a hurry to find the grave.

Asma took him by the hand, took him over to the watering hose, which lay on the ground. She raised the hose, wound the tube around his neck, hung it over his shoulder, and placed the nozzle in his right hand.

"That way, you can manage."

Then, she went with him to the water faucet.

"You'll water the graves that need it and then the main pathway. But don't squander it. Water's more expensive than diamonds! . . . so, do you think you can take care of it?"

"I can," said the child.

Feeling she could have confidence in him, she showed him where he could find his parents' grave once the work was done.

"When you've finished the watering, you'll find it at the far end of the cemetery below a fallen wall. You'll recognize the stone where your grandfather carved their initials."

"I'll recognize it."

Despite the ruins around him, thanks to the water, Omar-Jo was going to be in a state of euphoria for a few minutes.

Now controlling the opening of the hose, now freeing it, he squirted out a thin trickle or a torrent, a stream or a waterfall.

He delighted in reviving the grass, bringing the greenery,

drooping at half-mast, back to life, inundating the stagnant roots. He flushed away the dust that covered the marble stones with a blackish shroud, bringing their veins and their brightness to the surface. The artificial flowers sparkled, mud puddles changed into ponds; a few crows rushed over, wetting their wings and splashing about.

With total disregard for economy, Omar-Jo flooded the arid and bruised land with water, which it drank up immediately. Sharing that thirst, that desire, he moistened his face, sprinkled water on his head and neck, drenched his body. Then, with his mouth wide open, he drank great gulps of that effervescent water.

A little later, the child had no trouble recognizing the marble square with the initials of Omar and Annette under the date of their eternal union, 1987.

Omar-Jo controlled the water with his fingers, so it flowed in a fine rain, in caresses on the entwined initials.

Finally, he knelt down; he placed his cheek on the flat stone.

His face was wet with fresh water mixed with the salt water of his tears.

Omar-Jo would abandon the show, begin it again, as if there were no separation between one world and the other.

He would circulate around the Merry-go-round, go into the ever-increasing crowd. He would tease this person or that, brush their faces lightly with his yellow handkerchief or his cloth tulip; he would leave a large red smudge on a tiny tot's cheek with his kiss.

All the zanies, all the fools, all the graciosos, all the minstrels, the itinerant players, the white-faced circus clowns, the Monsieur Loyals, the Augustes, of times past and present, dwelt in his body, each in turn. Mixing impertinence and formalities, eloquence and devilish tricks, silence and acrobatics, he kept the attention of young and old. Sometimes, he tried to make Maxime his partner, but Maxime resisted the idea.

So the child used his feather duster as his interlocutor, insulting it or flattering it, before he flicked it, languorously, over his face. Omar-Jo knew how to communicate; even his alarming lapses seemed accepted by the public. He managed to slip into any age, as if he had passed through all of them, transforming his smooth, sweet-scented skin into a fragile, slack tissue in an instant.

"How do you know all that when you're only twelve?"

The child didn't know. His knowledge flashed from him as if each stage of existence had been imprinted on him at birth, as if youth, maturity, old age were already a part of his being. Not one of those ages was frightening or distasteful to him. He had only to think of the example of his grandfather Joseph, whose years mounted up to eighty-six, to judge the resources of old age.

One evening, just before closing time, Omar-Jo threw himself down on the platform on all fours, howling at the moon like a dog: "Solitude! . . . solitude! . . . come back tomorrow, my friends, come back."

Was that just extraordinary skill? wondered Maxime as, exhausted, he dropped beside Omar-Jo, legs dangling over the edge of the Merry-go-round. Side-by-side, the child and the proprietor shared a chocolate bar.

"Why that terrible cry? It breaks my heart."

"Don't worry, Maxime. You'll never be alone."

"What do *you* know about it?"

"You have me!"

"Oh?" said Maxime.

"And, *I've* got you."

"So that's how you see things?"

"That's the way things are."

"Anyway, it's your fault I won't have any vacation this summer: we're working."

"You mean we're playing," concluded the child.

FOR SOME TIME, Maxime had focused his attention on one young woman in her thirties out of all the carousel's customers. Strands of blond hair strayed from her chignon, placed high on her neck; she wore round, rimmed glasses with thin gold frames. She had an amiable, laughing face. A beauty mark above her upper lip gave her an impish air.

She changed her blouse every day but never her skirt. It was always the same one, flame red, flaring from the waist like a corolla and scarcely covering her knee. The carousel owner had nicknamed her the Poppy Woman.

Now, Maxime's appearance changed with the Merry-go-round's success. He had lost his paunch; he changed his shirt every morning; he smiled more often. The grandmothers who had considered him one of their own generation at the time of his defeat now treated him like an elder son or, at worst, like a much younger brother. Mothers, other women who brought children, again seemed nice to look at, appealing. When he passed among them to hand out tickets, he would joke or dare a wink at one or the other of them.

But he still preferred the Poppy Woman. The little girl she held by the hand when she arrived had primped curls and was enveloped in a pink percale dress. She wore high, white lisle socks, patent-leather Mary Janes. Her stiffness was in sharp contrast to her companion's natural and relaxed manner.

Both of them spent the greater part of the afternoon at the Merry-go-round. No sooner did one turn end than the little girl called for another in a commanding, petulant voice. There was no end to it, especially since she got what she wanted right away.

Back on the ground again, she demanded—immediately—a balloon or a top or cotton candy—all sold in the next shop. Back again, she ordered one more time around.

"It's late. This will be the last one, Thérèse."

The child paid no heed to warnings. She climbed on the platform again, picked out the horse she must have, and drove off the horse's first occupant, if there was one.

Omar-Jo observed her from a distance.

As soon as the Merry-go-round started to move, a complete metamorphosis took place. Bent forward from the waist, her cheek against the animal's neck, Thérèse seemed to race hell-bent for election. Her curls relaxed, her lips loosened. Her mouth opened; she breathed in the wind. Imagining space, she forgot herself.

With one leap, Omar-Jo landed on the horse next to hers. Trying to compete with the insolent equestrienne, he raised one leg to a horizontal position, found his balance.

She stared at him in wonderment.

"I'm just as good as you. But on a real horse. My father owns a stable."

The Poppy Woman never let the child out of her sight. For more than a week, she had gone along with her whims, so she could attend Omar-Jo's show. She had seen some of his costumes, some of his interpretations. Again, yesterday, he'd strolled around as Charlot, a small, heartrending, and somber form, suddenly coming out from among the gaudy mounts.

He had drawn the famous mustache with a piece of coal; he had acquired the knot of a black tie and even a round hat. His extremely long jacket sleeves hid the absence of his left arm. With his other, he gave a jaunty twirl to a branch whittled into a cane.

When he spoke, his words were a magical murmur of several languages mixed together. Then, suddenly, he would raise his voice:

> *I live in all the earth*
> *My laughter or my tears*
> *Are for the faraway*
> *For the now and here*
> *For the small For the great*
> *I live beneath the earth*
> *From which I shall never*
> *disappear.*

When he passed close to Thérèse, she would reach out her hand to catch hold of his clothes, as if to be certain he truly existed. But he escaped her grasp every time.

"One more time," the little girl insisted.

The Poppy Woman searched her purse. "I don't have any more money, Thérèse. Only bus tickets to get home."

Convinced that her determination would bring a miracle, the girl paid no attention at all to the answer she had just heard.

"One last time. Hurry up, the Merry-go-round's going to leave," she went on as she stamped her foot.

"Is this child yours?" asked Maxime.

"Yes," said the woman as she rummaged around feverishly in her purse.

"Stop looking."

He seized the child by her waist, raised her up, and set her down astride the chestnut horse.

The Poppy Woman apologized profusely. "I'll pay you back tomorrow, without fail."

"It's gratis."

"Gratis? . . . but why free?"

"It's my pleasure."

He had liked making the gesture. He repeated, "Gratis, gratis . . ." to savor the word. Right away, he wondered if it was a spontaneous gesture or if he'd made it simply in expectation of favors.

Pulling her glasses down to the end of her nose, she showed him her mischievous blue gray eyes.

"My name is Maxime."

"Like Saint Maxima?"

"But *I'm* not a saint. Far from it."

He suddenly remembered — an irritating memory — Odile, a talkative, clinging, ugly classmate of his. Year after year, she sent him her good wishes on his name day, cards so insipid they made him feel like getting away from all the saints, the apostles, and those of the Roman Church, and calling himself Omar or Levi, for example.

"Call me Max," he suggested.

She went on without hesitation.

"Your little boy is wonderful. If I were in the movies, I'd hire him immediately."

"He isn't my son. But like a son to me," he hastened to add.

"I've never seen anything more tragic and funnier than that child! I come back every afternoon."

"I'd noticed."

It was getting late, the Merry-go-round was just starting on its last rides. The greater part of the public had scattered.

Seeing a bushy mop of hair through the glass, Maxime called out toward the booth, "Omar-Jo, when you're dressed again, come here. We're waiting for you!"

That day, the child was taking off a matador's suit of lights, decorated in harlequin colors.

Coming out of the booth, his body suddenly seemed very frail and sickly, like a butterfly with singed wings. His stump poked out of his T-shirt sleeve.

There were long brownish streaks of greasepaint left on his cheeks.

"Do you know what the lady's just told me? That you should be in the movies."

"Life is the movies."

"Where do you come from?" asked the woman.

"Everywhere."

"I thought so."

They seemed to understand each other without explanations.

"What's your name?" asked the child.

"Cher because of my mother, an American. And Anne. My father was French."

"You have a double name, like me."

"Yes, like you. But they usually call me Cher."

Maxime went off to shut down the Merry-go-round and to make Thérèse get off. Glued to her horse, almost alone, she was taking her last turns.

"My mother's name was Annette," said Omar-Jo. "Anne, Annette, they're about the same."

He stared at her, compared one young woman to the other for a moment. They didn't look the least bit alike.

"I'm glad I have the same name as your mother."

He liked the sound of her voice. Her simplicity too. And the gaiety that bubbled from her.

"I'll call you Cheranne."

"Cher and Anne. The two together?"

"No. Cheranne. Only one word."

D

ear Grandfather,

Right now I'm living on a Merry-go-round. You'll like it a lot. I'm telling you about it because you'll come to see me soon, I'm sure. Your saber dance will have a marvelous effect if you do it amidst the wooden horses. All the little children will clap for you. Later, when I'm big, I'll buy the Merry-go-round. It'll belong to both of us.

I don't see Antoine and Rosie a lot; they're very busy. As you know, business takes time. They've been on vacation for a few days; they needed it. We, they and I, came to the agreement that I could stay here.

Don't worry, Grandfather, I have friends. First of all, there's the carousel owner: his name is Maxime. Maxime, like the saint; but he's no saint! He growls too much and for no good reason. But it doesn't last. Though he's never said so, I think he likes me; and I like him too.

The name of the other person—I've just met her—is Cheranne. She makes me think of Annette, or maybe I say that because of their names, which are similar. Now that the country's calmer, you can take the plane and come here in a few hours. Do it in the fall. Lots of things are about to happen here, and the Merry-go-round will be even more beautiful! You will come, won't you? I'm waiting for you.

Your grandson who loves you,

Omar-Jo

Old Joseph had done his best to get the child to leave the country.

"At your age you must visit the whole world."

At first, Omar-Jo wouldn't hear of leaving. He clung to his grandfather, to the hospitable, warm village people. He feared that if he went to another place, his memories of his parents would fade.

"Omar and Annette will never be erased from your memory; they will always live in you. Don't stay cooped up here, Omar-Jo. You were born in the war, you mustn't live in war. You must see the world, come to live in peace. Roots are exportable, you'll see. They mustn't suffocate you nor hold you back."

"Grandfather, you never left?"

"I couldn't, circumstances . . . but my mind *did* travel a lot!"

"Mine travels too."

"That shouldn't be enough for you, my child. Your eyes need other horizons."

"I'll be so alone, far away from you."

"Knowing you, knowing us, you and I will never be alone. But you'll always keep a small, solitary space deep down inside yourself, because you're like that, because you need that to find yourself again. You used to tell your parents sometimes, 'Act as if I'm not there.' Do you remember?"

"What will I do, out there, after I've finished school?"

"I've faith in you, Omar-Jo. You'll find something."

Joseph also told himself that a child mustn't share the life of an old man for too long. He had to face it; he'd grown old: his body no longer kept up with his passionate soul; his flesh was becoming less responsive to his trembling heart; hope had dulled. Omar-Jo ought to build in other ways, in other places, rather than on the past alone. And he must transform destructive images into images of the future.

Stubborn in his refusal, the child hung on his grandfather, dogging his footsteps for hours on end, from the cottage to the small garden to the land nearby.

Finally, he let himself be convinced. Since Joseph was illiterate, it was Omar-Jo who composed the first letter to Antoine and Rosie. Together, they waited for the answer.

A few days before leaving, the child lingered near the small plot of vines, absorbed in observation of an anthill. At twilight, he perched up among the branches of a large apple tree. From that spot, he gazed at the city. His city at the edge of the sea, surrounded by smiling hills. How innocent and joyous it seemed from so far away, from so high! The city, the murderous city.

Joseph would have liked to give Omar-Jo the ceremonial saber, his most precious possession. But the cumbersome package would complicate his trip.

The day before the boy left, he gave him a handful of dirt in a little plastic sack.

At the port, a few minutes before boarding, he slipped Omar's scarab ring on his grandson's ring finger.

"I'm leaving you," said the child, holding back his tears.

"You're taking me along," said the old man.

At fourteen, Annette had found her first job as a housekeeper in the home of Lysia, a widow who had emigrated from Egypt.

Ruined by recent laws affecting the confiscation of property, Lysia had taken the same trip as her ancestors but in the opposite direction. They had left Lebanon a hundred years before to flee local conflicts and famine; they had found refuge and their fortune in the land of the Nile and had become completely integrated.

The revolution of 1952 was to bring an end to glaring injustices. It had occurred peacefully, as befitted that tolerant and pacific country. Later, unexpected government measures had suddenly stricken certain families, depriving them of their property. Lysia had found herself in that group and had to abandon the villa inherited from her father. Her sumptuous residence, kept up by a bevy of servants, had kept afloat for several decades, outside of time, under her authoritarian yet benign supervision.

Her husband's photograph held the place of honor in every room of the villa. Fifty years before, the husband, crazy about boating, had disappeared at sea with other amateur sailors when his yacht sank leaving the port of Alexandria.

Lysia's eyes always filled with tears as she contemplated his portrait: "If only you were still here beside me, my poor Élie!" With time, the handsome young man resembled a grandson more than a husband. Gazing into the distance, he seemed to be trying to escape from the sumptuous residence and his ardent jailer.

Since her exile, Lysia had been living in a two-bedroom apartment in Beirut in a middle-priced building. Trying to bring her opulent past to life again, she had stuffed her cramped residence with the objects she had recovered: vases and plates from China, a Bokhara carpet, a Jansen original divan, jade knickknacks, Damascus glassware, her silver settings. It was difficult to move around in that space filled to overflowing. By this display, Lysia hoped to remind her visitors of her past splendor and to force them to show her the respect due a person of her rank.

With the same hope, she spent several hours in front of her mirror trying to reconstruct a face that had long since vanished.

Her vanity table, with its oval mirror in a frame of cherubs, was littered with jars and vials. Every morning, in Annette's presence, she went about her metamorphosis: gradually, she would bury her natural, pallid face, touching in its fragility, under creams and powders. From time to time, she spoke to the young maid, whose silent, discreet presence comforted her.

ANDRÉE CHEDID

"Do you realize, Annette? I had nine servants to help me; now you're all I have."

Stopping, she motioned to Annette to come closer and, patting her cheek, said, "But you're worth all of them put together. All of them."

The results of her multicolored makeup satisfied her. Except for the neck. She finally wrapped it in silk scarves or hid it under necklaces as Africans do.

Brushing her brassy yellowish hair, she confided other snatches of her past to Annette; she boasted of her successes, her social connections.

Suddenly, impatient with her recalcitrant hair—a hairdresser was beyond her means—she bound it up in a fuchsia turban.

"How do I look, Annette?" she would ask, indifferent to the answer. Then, sighing, she slipped paste gems, poor substitutes for her confiscated jewels, on her arms, on her fingers.

Annette felt compassion for Lysia, who kept up this pathetic struggle every day; she even felt rather attached to the thoughtless and tenacious, generous, petty old woman. Lysia would shower her with baubles and old-fashioned dresses, then take them back immediately. She provided her with a room, fed her copiously, gave her pocket money but never even suggested wages.

"What would you do with them? In my house, you have all you need!"

"Later on," said Lysia, "*I* will take care of finding you a husband."

"No. I don't want you to. Never!"

The emphatic, categorical "no" bewildered Lysia. She had probably misunderstood.

"You're probably right, Annette. It's too early, far too early, to think about that."

She didn't intend to rush things. This child could still be useful to her for a long time; the responsibility of a husband and children would upset their life together.

But Annette didn't drop the subject. "I mean that I'm the one who'll choose my husband. No one else."

Their two faces, one next to the other, were suddenly reflected in the oval mirror. Lysia stared with indescribable astonishment at the face of the girl, who was usually so conciliatory. What did life have in store for her? What memories would she accumulate for her old age?

The idea that youth—beautiful, brief youth—was lost on people who couldn't enjoy it or take advantage of it made her shiver. "What a waste!"

If only she had a second chance; if only she, Lysia, could be sixteen again! She would take those dull eyes, that long nose. Oh yes, to be young again, she would change places with Annette if she had to. Afterward, she would manage!

The old woman pushed back her chair, straightened up with difficulty. Her aching joints were painful. Standing, she was a scrawny scarecrow: a plaster mannequin's head at the end of a knotty stick.

Lysia didn't wear a bra or panties under her blue slip. Breasts, stomach, buttocks had shriveled up; there was

104   nothing shameless about her dried-up flesh anymore. She'd kept the habit of walking around undressed in the morning, coming and going as she had long ago—when her flesh was luscious and desirable—before the eyes of the servants, as if they were only shadows, asexual phantoms.

It had been five days, and the Poppy Woman hadn't reappeared. On her last afternoon, Maxime had to restrain himself from disciplining the unbearable little girl; he wondered anxiously if the mother and the child had certain characteristics in common. To his relief, he didn't find any.

"She must resemble her father!"

"What father? Who are you talking about?" asked Omar-Jo.

"That Thérèse. She gets her mother to do everything she wants. If she were mine . . ."

"Aren't you forgetting that you're the one who offered her a free ride?"

"It wasn't for that little bitch!"

"Oh? . . . Who was it for?"

"Don't look so innocent, Omar-Jo."

"By the way, what's her name?"

"Who are you talking about?"

"Well, her mother!"

"You talk to each other for hours on end. She certainly told you her name."

"Her name is Cheranne."

"Cheranne? You made that up."

"Call her Cheranne. Bet she'll answer."

"You've really got a lot of nerve, Omar-Jo. As soon as you like a stranger, you treat him like a friend. You talk to him as if he were your age!"

"Why waste time, Maxime? It's . . . life's too short."

"A twelve-year-old doesn't say things like that! Well, you must have deserved a few good thrashings yourself. Didn't your father ever give you one? You're not answering; you have trouble remembering. It probably wasn't very often. Too bad, it would have done you good!"

mar-Jo was only eight at the time. That evening, seated on the floor in front of the television, he refused to go to bed in spite of Annette's promptings.

More than an hour before, the gunfire had suddenly started up again. Recently, the illusory truce had lasted; in spite of sporadic clashes, life had returned to normal little by little.

That evening, the whistling of the bombs had been more insistent. Were hostilities beginning again? Omar and Annette were whispering, holding hands. Although it didn't really worry them—the neighborhood had always been open, accepting—their particular situation made them more vulnerable than others. They tried to speak to each other, then to telephone friends without upsetting the child.

"It's time to go to bed, Omar-Jo."

He didn't budge. He'd turned up the sound. His neck tense, head stretched forward, he tried to enter the picture, take refuge there, so he could escape the noise of the missiles. The whistle of the rocket launchers and the grumble of the cannons were coming closer.

Annette and Omar started to whisper again. At all costs, they had to get advice, maybe take refuge in a nearby shelter. Their building didn't have a basement.

"Let me look. Leave me alone!" exclaimed Omar-Jo.

Still seated, he slid forward on the floor until he was almost touching the screen.

Omar, ordinarily so calm, rushed over to his son. He picked him up, carried him under his arm to the nearest bedroom. Omar-Jo was struggling furiously.

Sitting down on the bed, Omar stretched the child out on his stomach and spanked him.

Omar-Jo was dumbfounded. His face raised, he stared at his mother, who was standing in the open doorway, as stunned as he was.

"That is the first and last time," said Omar after putting the child back on his feet. "We're not living in easy times. You have to learn to grow up even faster than ever, Omar-Jo."

He kissed him, hugged him close. The child felt his father's mustache scratch his cheek. His mother, who had come closer, ran her fingers through his hair.

"Nothing will happen to you. Nothing! . . . ever!" he begged.

"Nothing." said Omar.

"Nothing, nothing!" repeated Annette. "You mustn't get upset."

The number of shells that pounded the night seemed to diminish.

M y father gave me a spanking once. Only once."

"How about slaps? You weren't slapped?" asked Maxime.

"Nobody'd dare slap me. Nobody."

"Okay, don't get angry. But I can't really see the difference. You've been hit in either case, haven't you?"

"A slap is an insult."

With a shout of laughter, he went on: "Only I have the right to give me a slap. Look!"

He swatted himself with the flat of his hand several times on one cheek, then on the other. He was roaring with laughter; his cheeks were pink from the slaps.

"I've got it: you're warning me," said Maxime. "And you're going into your act again!"

"I defend myself as best I can, Uncle Maxime."

"*Uncle* Maxime?"

"I've adopted you!" he said before he pirouetted away.

They continued their dialogue over the tarp.

"So. *You've* adopted *me*. Thanks for telling me, Omar-Jo. Nothing surprises me anymore; with you, everything's topsy-turvy."

After a last entrechat, the child came back and planted himself before the proprietor.

"If I ever abandoned your Merry-go-round, here's what would happen to it . . ."

He stretched out his arm, then made an airplane with his hand and fingers: its wings and body. With humming and whistling sound effects, he flew the machine: it hedge-hopped, rose, and banked before it turned over, pulled up, then took a nosedive toward the ground, where it crashed in a deafening explosion.

"Braggart!" You're too damn proud!"

"You're righ,. Uncle Maxime. It's pride that holds me up. Which holds us up, over there."

IN THE EVENING, they left the Square together to go back to the proprietor's rooms.

When the night was mild, they went on foot, strolling along the Rue de Rivoli, taking a longer way, so they could go up the Boulevard Henri-IV and look in the shop windows of the Faubourg Saint-Antoine.

"How would you like it if we, both of us, were set up in a livingroom like this one?"

"Not much," said the child. "I prefer your coach."

Omar-Jo pulled Maxime along behind him. They went into one courtyard after another, unearthed an old well, a fountain, the Musketeers' staircase, a washhouse. The child discovered different alleyways, was amused by their names:

"Passage de l'Homme, du Cheval-Blanc, de la Bonne-Graine, de la Main-d'Or . . ."

"You're some kid. I'm learning about my neighborhood from you."

In the vicinity of the Merry-go-round, the child wanted to know what the four statues of the Châtelet theater's facade represented.

Maxime had to consult his guide. "They are Drama, Comedy, Dance, and Music."

"Someday I'll do all that!"

"All those things, all at the same time? You're very sure of yourself!"

"In our next show!"

"Our next show! . . . that's going a bit far, don't you think, Omar-Jo?"

At other times, they would stop along the way, sit on a public bench, eat a sandwich with a beer or a lemonade.

It was there, one evening, that Omar-Jo translated a letter that his grandfather had addressed to Maxime.

My friend Maxime, for my grandson, thank you!

I will come to see your Merry-go-round someday.
In the meantime, it's turning around in my head. I
love it dearly, and I decorate it with all the fruits of
my garden. Sometimes, it goes up like a flying
saucer and hovers, or whirls around just above my
head.

Our days have been calm for some time. Public transportation has been restored, mail service has started up again. I think I can ship you some apricots and peaches soon. They will be a treat.

Our lives, our own Merry-go-round, are still crumbling in ruins, but now that the guns are silent, we'll manage to link up, to find each other again. Things must turn around someday! Our people must get on the same Merry-go-round again, one that will start out, go forward to a music of hope. Do you understand me, Maxime? You know I'm not dreaming? Remember your own wars and the terrible Occupation . . .

Omar-Jo has probably told you that I don't know how to write. The teacher from a village close to ours came just to write this letter. But the signature will be mine. You will find it at the bottom of the page. It's my thumbprint, with a bit of dirt in the creases.

Thank you, friend Maxime. The child had to live in a world at peace.

"Give me that letter; I want to keep it," said the carousel owner.

The child placed his lips on the thumbprint. Then he held it out to him.

SOMETIMES, Maxime and the child ate dinner on a café terrace.

"Tonight, it's your turn to choose the place, Omar-Jo."

They stopped in front of the Brasserie des Trois Portes.
Maxime scrutinized the menu posted outside.

"Come on, come on. Quick."

The child was pulling him by the arm.

"Let me look at the menu. If it's not too expensive, we'll go in."

"We'll go in anyway."

"You're not going to order me around."

"You said, 'It's your turn to choose tonight.' I've chosen: we're going in."

He pulled him over to the window with the raised curtain.

"Look. There in the back. You see?"

"I see all kinds of people."

"Over to the right. The red skirt, the black apron . . . the woman holding the big tray."

"The Poppy Woman!"

"Right. You were talking about her a little while ago. So, are we going in?"

Maxime followed the child. Going ahead of Maxime, Omar-Jo spotted a table in her service area.

"At this hour, Thérèse is sure to be in bed. You'll have the Poppy Woman all to yourself."

"You'll keep your share, I'm sure, Omar-Jo."

"I'll have Cheranne."

Annette had suffered from the absence of her mother, whom she had never known, and of her grandmother, who had disappeared too soon. In spite of Joseph's solicitude, she had always missed the company of women. Since she had come to know Lysia, she had transferred part of her repressed tenderness to the old woman. She was attentive to her innumerable needs and shared the same affinities, the same antipathies.

Lysia was hurt that she couldn't invite everyone who dropped by to meals; her means no longer permitted it. Since she could only offer coffee, tea, or lemonade, Annette took pains to present the tray with a lace mat or a cut flower, to supplement the drinks with preserves or coffee she had made.

Lysia had a cousin, Élise, who had no financial restrictions or difficulties, having emigrated some years before. Both she and her husband, Émile, a clever businessman who had been able to export a large part of their fortune, lived luxuriously in a nearby suburb overlooking the port

city. Although she felt affection for her cousin, Lysia could-
n't help but envy her.

"If your Élie hadn't died, you'd have been in the same
situation, Lysia. Without a husband to take care of her
finances, a woman isn't much good. I tell you, if I hadn't had
Émile . . ."

Émile, with his assertive portliness and British elegance,
continued to live a life of leisure and made their money
multiply. He devoted his days to drawing charts and graphs
that permitted him to follow the stock market quotations of
their various investments. A discriminating gourmet, he gave
instructions to the chef. In the afternoon, with the help of
his gardener, he took care of his flowers. He had even pro-
duced a new variegated rose named Émiliote, a prizewinner
in several competitions. When roses were in season, he
offered one rose, holding it by its long stem, to each of his
departing guests.

In addition to the gardener and his helpers and the
chauffeur, a Sudanese brought from Egypt, the couple had
another servant, a young woman in her thirties, who was a
deaf-mute.

Zékié had an oval Madonna face, a sensual mouth, green
eyes. Her dark, shining braids were coiled and pinned up
over her ears. She usually wore a black dress, black stockings, patent-leather T-strap shoes. And she always had on an
impeccable white, starched apron, as well as a stiff cap of
the same material. She put on white net gloves to serve at
the table.

Lysia, more haphazard, would never have required such

a livery of Annette, or perhaps she had a feeling the girl wouldn't have accepted an accoutrement like that.

Apparently, Zékié conformed. Her face remained unperturbed; her smile, almost too affable. But sometimes, Annette caught a glimpse of the flashes of hatred that filtered into Zékié's eyes. Their brief, burning fury pierced her muteness and that mask of sweetness.

Uncaring, inattentive, the couple noticed nothing. Without consideration for the young woman, Élise reprimanded her with gestures in front of others. Émile, overly particular, found fault with her constantly, miming how she ought to have acted.

Zékié's only response was to lower her head humbly, hiding her resentment deep in the pupils of her eyes.

During meals, Annette stayed very close to Lysia, watching for the slightest signal, giving her her pills, covering her shoulders with a shawl if the need should arise.

"That Zékié is a witch!" Élise commented, lowering her voice. "I've surprised her several times in the gardener's company: a married man with a wife and five children! He joins them in the mountains every Sunday, but during the week he sleeps here. Émile, I'm sure shameful things are going on under our roof."

Her husband's indifference whenever she brought up the subject irritated her, and she finally wondered if he too hadn't had the benefit of the depraved woman's favors.

"She does her work well," explained Émile.

"We'd certainly have problems if she became pregnant."

"We'd send her back to her family, that's all."

"And you know how she'd be received in her village!"

"That's her problem."

During the entire conversation, the deaf-mute's face remained impassive. Annette watched her in anguish, wondering if certain of those words hadn't filtered through her blocked ears, wounding her. Annette also had anxious thoughts about her future child. How, by whom would he come to her?

While Émile was taking a siesta, Élise opened up her closets in honor of her cousin.

"I'm going to show you everything."

Used to this kind of display, Zékié exhibited dresses, coats, and furs. She held them high, still on their hangers, one after the other, disappearing behind each garment she showed.

"An ermine cape by Révillon," recited Élise. "A Maggy Rouff dress, a Vionnet negligee. Did you notice those armholes?. . . blue mink collar, astrakhan jacket, suit by Chanel. It's cut beautifully! A jacket by Schiaparelli . . . come closer, see how those buttons are done?"

"How did you manage to save these marvelous things?" sighed Lysia. In her ready-made skirt and blouse, she felt diminished, deprived. Calling Annette to her rescue, she whispered in her ear, "She doesn't realize that's all in the past!"

IN '74, TWO YEARS after that visit, hostilities broke out. In '77, the villa was sacked: knickknacks, crystal, dishes broken to bits; carpets and furniture ripped and burned. The motive of the devastation seemed vengeance, not pillage.

In front of the wardrobe, smashed open, clothes and furs, cut to shreds with maniacal care, were piled in pathetic heaps. In the back of one of the closets, they found Élise's corpse wrapped in her sable coat, with a fox collar tight around her neck. Émile's machine-gunned body lay in the garden in the midst of his Émiliotes. The newspapers spared no details.

Because of the letter *Z*, carved angrily into the woodwork, suspicion fell on the deaf-mute. Not a trace of her was found. Nor of the gardener, either. His wife waited for him in vain, for years.

It was long before this drama, a few months after the last meal at her cousin's—peace still prevailed—that Lysia, accompanied by Annette, took flight to Egypt.

The child and the carousel owner elbowed their way through the smoky, noisy room to seats in the back of the brasserie. Much of the restaurant was visible from their table, as well as the swinging doors into the kitchen, which swept open, shut, constantly, at a precipitant rate.

Cheranne, who was taking the orders of a group of tourists, hadn't spotted them yet.

"Motion to her," prompted Omar-Jo.

Scarcely over his surprise, Maxime tried to hide his excitement. Impatient, the child straightened up in his chair. Before Maxime could restrain him, he called out over the diners' heads, "Cheranne! Cheranne! It's us!"

It took several seconds for the young woman to remember her new name. As soon as she caught sight of Omar-Jo, she recognized him; her face lit up. She stood up on tiptoe and raised her hand in answer to their greeting.

"I'm coming!" she exclaimed.

Gripped by a feeling she hadn't had for a long time, she hurried to finish up the orders.

"Are you happy, Maxime?" asked the child as he saw her approaching.

"It's the first time I've set foot in this place."

"What about Cheranne? What do you think of her? . . . aren't you going to answer? You offered her a free ride. That's not like you."

"How do you know what I'm like?"

"You're a real tightwad, aren't you?"

"My parents slaved away their lives."

"Mine, too."

Cheranne's arms were already around the child. "I've been expecting to see you."

Under the bright ceiling lights, Maxime noticed her few wrinkles, then the dimple in her chin, which gave her a youthful air. Her gray blue eyes sparkled behind her glasses.

"I'll stand you an aperitif!"

Her shell white skin smelled of lavender.

"Have you been working here a long time?" asked Maxime.

"Evenings. I'm filling in."

"And your little girl?"

"She's not mine. I show her around on days off, that's all."

The carousel proprietor felt quite relieved that the terrible Thérèse was not related to the young woman.

"It's thanks to her that I discovered you, Omar-Jo."

The boy was the center of attention for her.

"Do you have any children?"

"I couldn't have any. That's all for the best, since I'm divorced."

Maxime didn't dare ask her any more questions.

"You'll become a great comic, Omar-Jo," Cheranne continued. She stroked his stump fondly. "You'll even turn this to your advantage."

Then, she turned to Maxime: "I'll come back to sit with you when I'm through serving, if you'll wait for me. I'll sing one of my songs, Omar-Jo."

"One of your songs?"

"I do the words; my friend Sugar composes the music."

Maxime had a questioning look.

"Sugar is a real musician, a black from Los Angeles. He's been living in Paris for the last two years."

"You sing in which language?"

"In both. My mother is American."

AS SOON AS her father died, Cheranne, who was twelve, had returned to the United States with her mother. Harriet had gone back to her family in a town in Florida. She had never adapted to exile.

The opposite of her mother, Cheranne thought only of going back to Paris. Her marriage with Steve had delayed the return. Since her divorce, she had come back to Paris to live in her native city, trying, with some difficulty, to earn her living there.

The break with Steve had taken place more than two years earlier. At times, Steve would suddenly reappear in her life. Cheranne was both happy and tormented when he turned up.

Shortly after the luncheon at her cousin's, Lysia received a letter from her lawyer. He assured her there was a good chance she would get back part of her property or at least receive some compensation. She decided to take the trip to Egypt in Annette's company.

In Cairo, she stayed at the home of a childhood friend. Because the rent remained so modest, Laurice continued to live in her nine-room apartment. But, since she no longer had the means to keep it up, it was gradually going to ruin. Some of the parquet was missing; the worn carpets were threadbare; wall hangings were unraveled; armchairs and divans, their padding full of holes, had lost an arm or a leg. Most of the chandeliers had a few crystal pieces missing; the sconces were askew on the peeling walls. Everything exuded dust and neglect.

On the few wintry days, they shook with cold in those vast residences. Laurice had placed a cylindrical portable gas stove in Lysia's room. To eliminate the odor and humidify the air, on top of the stove there was a pan of water in which eucalyptus leaves floated.

Every afternoon, Laurice got ten or so friends together around card tables for endless games of bridge or pinochle. The hostess provided drinks; the guests brought sweets or cigarettes. Since they could no longer play for money, they took turns furnishing the winners' prizes: a pair of nylons from the precious stock they'd hoarded, a lawn handkerchief, a pair of gloves, samples of perfume from Paris.

Lysia was both irritated and pleased when she went back to that small outmoded world. There were always the same jokes, the same petty quarrels, the same gossip, the same superficial niceties. In addition, there were a litany of complaints, endless sighs for the past, to which they attributed extravagant charms. The mirage—more and more illusory, mythical—of a return to the old days, of recovering their fortunes, gave a spark to their limited existence and kept their taste for the future alive. Stagnating like the women, certain brothers and husbands wasted their last years in endless lawsuits.

Lysia didn't envy their way of life and was glad she had escaped it. She didn't wish to take possession of her villa again or live in one of those immense dusty apartments hidden away in disintegrating buildings.

The day before, when she had been caught in an elevator that had suddenly broken down for two hours, she had sworn she would walk up from then on. Since that day, panting, leaning on Annette's arm, she had climbed up the six floors.

"Our two-room apartment is better than this, don't you think?"

Her view of things seemed to change. She felt closer to

Annette than to her former friends. She reproached herself for her selfishness toward the child, who had just turned twenty—the high point of youth! Annette's inevitable decline would follow, as does everyone's. In spite of the girl's defiance, Lysia would have to take care of finding her a husband. As soon as she got back, she would talk seriously to Joseph about it.

DOWN ON THE SIDEWALK outside the building, Lysia hailed a taxi to go to her lawyer's.

In the streets, on the sidewalks, a swarming mass advanced slowly and good-naturedly. Sometimes, internal pressure alone blocked their movement.

Annette felt an instinctive sympathy for the people of this city with their sorrow and smiles, indigence and cunning. The car crept along. She noticed a corpulent woman in a gaudy dress, who stared at her with bright eyes; a tiny child with a circle of flies around his eyes, who was astride the shoulders of his mother, dressed in black. A hunchbacked beggar, wisdom in his eyes, put out his hand to her. A heavy, wheezing man with a small brown case clutched to his chest hesitated, huffing, on the side of the road, before he plunged into the multitude. Innumerable young faces dotted the teeming parade.

The chauffeur kept calm, drove smoothly. In few words, with an innate reserve, he explained his city, the pressing problems that beset it. Concerned with the old woman's comfort, he would turn around from time to time. "Are you all right?"

As they drove along, Lysia asked him if he would be free

during their two-week stay. They rapidly agreed on a price
and where they would meet each day.

"What's your name?"

"Omar."

"I can trust him," she murmured, leaning toward
Annette. "I can size up a person at first glance."

Omar was dressed in an open-collared checked shirt and
gray pants. He had a swarthy complexion; thick, curly hair;
large black eyes; an imposing stature, which he seemed
apologetic about. He radiated kindness and calm.

His eyes met Annette's several times in the rearview
mirror. What they both felt when that happened was so new
to them that they were ill at ease.

It was after midnight when Cheranne came to sit down at their table. Wisps of hair hung over her forehead; she was even more pallid than before; the circles that stood out under her eyes were even darker.

She put her elbows on the table, buried her face in her hands.

"Just a few minutes, and I'll be okay."

Both of them looked at her without a word. Their silent presence did her good.

Cheranne finally raised her head. Without opening her eyes, she put out her hand to the child's cheek and ran her fingers over it as a blind man would. His firm flesh under soft, smooth-textured skin, the pulse of fresh blood at his temples helped her emerge from her fatigue.

"It's Omar-Jo who caught sight of you first. It was his idea to come in," said the carousel owner. "He was sure we wouldn't bother you."

"He was right."

She opened her eyes, looked at the child, and said in a warm voice, "You have the best eyes in the world, little clown!"

One word, one gesture—these were enough to bring back memories. There was no pain in Omar-Jo this time, only the joy of happiness relived.

The now empty brasserie was still full of smoke, of warmth, and of the traces of all the voices that had once intermingled there in an indescribable din.

The waiters clearing the tables moved in a precise, efficient ballet; later, they set up the same tables for the following day.

Maxime was placing a circle of soft bread pellets around his plate.

"It's nice out tonight. Let's the three of us go for a walk," suggested Cheranne.

With them, she would make up for the time she'd lost so far away from this city. With them, she would rediscover Paris. She would forget that part of her childhood buried in banal, comfortable suburbs on the other side of the Atlantic.

HER MOTHER, Harriet, had met Jacques in Paris when she arrived in France with a student group. They had married in less than a week. The couple had never gotten along. Because of their infant daughter, their union, a series of separations and reconciliations, lasted ten years. Cher could still hear the shouting that kept her awake and in tears all night.

Ill at ease in the capital, whose people she thought

mocking and inhospitable, Harriet tried hard, albeit unsuccessfully, to inspire nostalgia for her own land in her child. She constantly evoked its glorious, sparkling bay, the countless sunny days, the conviviality of its inhabitants. She filled her stories with animals who lived there: dolphins who could speak, dancing whales, motionless crocodiles, bright butterflies, herons with long, long legs, tortoises of all shapes and sizes, manatees with their abundant udders, owls, lizards, pelicans.

The child listened to the tales with indifference, trying to turn from these stories of other places to the secrets and legends of Paris.

As soon as Harriet divorced, she brought little Cher back to Arosville, a small town on the Gulf of Mexico, which spread out over several miles. The child was almost eleven.

Cheranne was to take the same voyage across the Atlantic as her mother had but in the opposite direction. She promised herself she would go back to her native city once she was an adult. Meeting Steve had delayed the reunion for several years.

"DO YOU feel better?" asked Maxime.

Cheranne lifted her head, cleared her throat, and began to sing in a low voice:

For my most faithful friend
I grow a white, white rose
In July as in December.

"It's a southern song. One of my mother's."

For the cruel friend
Who betrays my heart
I grow neither thorns nor briers,
But a white, white rose instead.

While she was pronouncing these last words, Steve's image came to the fore, dispelling all other feelings. In spite of their separation, she couldn't forget him.

She turned suddenly to Omar-Jo.

"I can sing you one of my own songs, if you want."

"Your songs?"

She pulled a wad of papers and colored pencils out of her apron pocket, which she scattered over the yellow tablecloth. Her pages were like scraps of material pieced together in all directions.

"Your writing . . . it looks like symbols, like ancient pictographs . . . ," remarked Maxime.

"I'm part Indian," she said. "But, Omar-Jo, you come from an even greater distance in time!"

Again, Maxime felt excluded from their dialogue. The child touched his shoulder.

"We're all here in your country, Maxime. In your country, in mine, in ours!" he crooned.

The *forain* smiled at him and asked if they shouldn't celebrate their coming together with a drink.

"It's my round," said Cheranne, calling young Fernand, who was just finishing his shift.

"Read us your songs," asked Omar-Jo.

"You won't make fun of me, will you, Maxime?"

He had no intention of poking fun. When he was near Cheranne, he was defenseless. He could not resist the happiness that swept through him, a happiness he had never shared with any woman.

"You always have a slightly sardonic look," she continued, smiling.

The child intervened: "Maxime is a poet. Who else but a poet would have dropped everything to buy himself a Merry-go-round? Who else would have chosen a clown, a foreigner, a cripple as his companion?"

"You always exaggerate," said the *forain*.

"Aren't I your companion?"

"That's not what I meant."

"Omar-Jo's right," interrupted Cheranne. "Who else but Maxime?"

With their drinks, all three became a bit tipsy. Cheranne took hold of Maxime's left hand, the child's right.

"It's a ring. To life! To death!"

To close the circle, Maxime looked for Omar-Jo's other hand. Then, suddenly embarrassed at his blunder, he put his arms around the child's shoulder and hugged him to himself.

"Here's to life, to death! To death, to life!"

They swung back and forth that way for a long moment, repeating in unison: "To life, to death! To death, to life!"

It was while they were singing this song that, for the first time, Maxime thought of giving a prosthesis to Omar-Jo.

Next, Cheranne sang her own songs. The unusual words were all of love, of vulnerable and illusory loves, of miracles and heartbreak.

The lights had gone out. The waiter Fernand had lit a candle, stuck it in a brown jar encrusted with granular melted wax, set the jar in the center of the table. Then, he'd gone away on tiptoe.

"To death! To life!" Again, they took up the refrain.

With a circle of shadows around them, all three seemed to be floating on an island or on a tiny ship at sea. Their own moving shadows, joined together and cast upward, danced upon the ceiling.

"And the music?" asked Omar-Jo.

"The music. It's Sugar's. I'll introduce him to you."

Maxime pressed Cheranne's fingers. She responded. They glanced at each other.

Fernand ran in, dressed in his street clothes.

"You're wanted on the telephone, Cher. It's long distance."

The young woman tore her hand away from Maxime's, jumped up, stuffed her batch of songs into her pocket, and ran toward the phone booth.

"You'll come back?" called the child.

She didn't turn around.

Lysia made up for her years of skimping by buying out the shops. Yet, her financial manager had advised her to be economical: although things had improved, her resources were still modest. When she looked in her mirror, her eyesight—which she was careful not to correct with glasses—reflected a flattering, blurred image. Seeing herself as she wished to be seen, she found it hard to resist buying garish spring outfits: she came back to Laurice's every evening loaded down with packages.

A generous woman, she also showered her hostess with gifts. She brought back a crocodile handbag for her cousin Élise, both to thank her for meals she'd had at the villa and to impress her with her own new financial situation. Four years later, the same handbag was found in the ruins of the ravaged villa. It held a valuable ring and a bundle of bank notes; yet, it hadn't been opened.

When their stay was about half over, she didn't have enough left to buy Annette something to wear. Annette was relieved; the old lady would have decided to give her a garment in which she would be ill at ease—a frilly skirt and

blouse, for example, or an almost monkish outfit, depend-   133
ing on how she felt.

At the end of the afternoon, when the light became less cor-
rosive and the heat was dissipating, Lysia and one of her
friends would settle into the rear seat of the car.

"Take us for a nice ride, Omar!"

She left the choice of their destination up to the chauffeur. Annette would take a seat beside him. The two women
would chitchat in the backseat, oblivious to what was going
on outside the car windows.

Omar spoke only for Annette. He showed her the City
of the Dead, Old Cairo, then went off in the direction of the
pyramids, the dam, Matarieh: "On their flight into Egypt,
Mary, Joseph, and the baby Jesus found refuge here under
a tree. We Muslims too revere this place."

He often turned off on country roads that reminded him
of his own village, feeling as though he wanted her—he
didn't know why—to love and smell his own soil, rub it
between her fingers.

He would repeat the same few words: "See, over there.
Look to your left. That village, this canal, those fields . . . farther away, the desert . . . all that's so beautiful! Does it look
like your country?"

She shook her head no. She didn't see any similarity
between the hills she knew, her own radiant mountains, her
ocean—so very blue, visible from almost everywhere—and
this slow, sweeping river, the bright green stretches of open
land so rapidly hemmed in by sandy cliffs.

She didn't see any comparison between the majestic
Nile and the lively springs or rushing streams of her moun-

tain. The age-old banyans sitting on their brood of abiding roots were unrelated to the tall sea pines graced with ever-changing branches. The patient feluccas were scarcely comparable to her bold fishing boats.

He repeated the question: "Does it look like your country?"

"Both are beautiful and so are alike," she said suddenly.

"Yes, that's it, beauty," he went on. "Beauty . . ."

He showed her a cardboard box of books under his seat.

"I'm educating myself. There are so many problems here and in the world. I want to learn, know. If you like, I'll pass my readings on to you."

"We'll be leaving soon," she answered.

At other times, he pointed out mud houses, called her attention to women in clothes like those of centuries past, who beat their laundry on canal banks; naked, laughing children mounted on the backs of water buffalo. Peasants, their feet deep in mud, turned over soil that belonged to others. Instantly, Annette thought of her father, Joseph, who owned a patch of ground all his own.

She imagined them face-to-face: the old man—flamboyant, garrulous, always on the go—and this young man shaped out of clay and silences. "So unalike," she pondered. Yet, there was something similar about them; she didn't know exactly what.

The day they were to leave, the chauffeur had gone up to get the suitcases.

Lysia was telephoning. Annette was leaning on the windowsill.

"I'll miss this country," she said without turning around.

"It will miss you," said Omar, a few steps behind the young woman.

Unaware of what was happening between the two young people, Lysia, at a peak of excitement—her lawyer had just informed her that her monthly allocation would be doubled—rushed toward Omar: "I need a full-time chauffeur; would you come to our country? We'll sign a one-year contract, we'll take care of your papers. Do you agree?"

That took Annette's breath away. She ran from the room so she couldn't hear the answer.

A FEW MONTHS later, when Annette and Omar announced they intended to marry, Lysia was staggered. Her mouth dropped open; then she went into a fit of rage. Hopping mad and feeling guilty because she'd brought them together, she threatened:

"You're leaving! You're leaving right away next week, Omar. And I had confidence in you!"

Did they realize the problems their marriage was going to cause, that there was nothing they could do about their situation?

"I would never have thought it of you, Annette! What's your poor father going to say? Do you want to kill him?"

Without hesitation, old Joseph asked to meet Omar alone.

Omar stopped his car at the entrance to the village and went on by foot. The curious were already at their windows.

136 He went around the church, into the little garden, pulled the cord that set off the tinkling bell.

The old man was not long in coming.

They liked each other instantly.

After a few minutes, they set each other laughing. They took a turn in the orchard, shared the same meal. Their love for Annette did the rest.

Convinced that God's heart was vast enough to hold all the believers in the world—past, present, and future, even nonbelievers like himself—Joseph took it upon himself to convince first those close to him, then the community, which already claimed five different sects.

He succeeded. The two men had a gift in common: they could arouse sympathy.

Invited to the marriage a little while later, Lysia congratulated herself on being the instigator of the "happy event."

"A fine example of cohabitation!" she proclaimed.

That was in 1973, just before the war broke out. Omar-Jo was to be born three years later in a divided and wounded land. The people thought it was impossible for such a state of war and tension to last.

S teve's voice on the line came from far away and faded in and out. Cheranne gave a long look out into the brasserie, caught sight of the only lighted table, where Maxime and Omar-Jo were sitting side by side. She closed the phone-booth door to hear better.

In spite of their separation, Cheranne and Steve kept track of each other. They always knew how to get in touch.

Steve had abandoned his career in sports, which he was sometimes sorry he hadn't pursued further; at moments, he blamed his wife for that. Since then, changing to business, he seemed satisfied; the boldness of his plans and the attraction of the money motivated him.

He asked her for news on the phone, announced his immediate arrival, and told her he wanted to see her again.

While she listened to him, she remembered their last meeting almost a year before. Tired from a long trip, Steve had slept at her place. They always got together again with the same youthful enthusiasm, but things soured very quickly. In their conversations, Steve's constant irony cut short her sentences. But stretched out beside each other, the silent closeness of their bodies seemed to bind them together again.

That night, Steve had moaned in his sleep; she didn't know why. Each had gone a different way, so their lives had drifted apart little by little; yet, Cheranne couldn't bear the thought that Steve might be unhappy.

She pulled the sheet up over their heads, circled his broad shoulders with her arm; he still complained, sighing in his dream. She placed her chest against Steve's back, twined her legs with his, giving him her warmth. With her ear tight against his shoulder blades, unmoving, she pressed him close to her, waiting for his breathing to slow.

All was calm again. He turned over without waking from his sleep. She too slept, holding his hand.

At other times, it was he who dispelled her worries with a few words, a few caresses. In spite of their differences, in some inexplicable way they were able to comfort each other.

Cheranne glanced furtively toward the dining room. Maxime and Omar-Jo seemed to move in another universe far away from her. She turned away from them and, gripping the phone in both hands, she said, "It's good to hear your voice, Steve."

"Do you usually work so late?" he asked.

"I was with friends."

There was silence.

She imagined what Steve's reaction to the *forain* and the child would be if he were to meet them face-to-face; he would have told her that she only liked and spent time with "nobodies, cripples."

"At least your songs have been published, haven't they?"

"Not yet."

She felt his mocking look and wanted to run away. He kept her there by telling her about his many travels in the United States and other foreign countries.

"Are you happy? Is your business going well?"

"Why bother to talk to you about it?" he cut in. "You wouldn't understand a thing."

She wished he could confide in her. Maybe it was her fault? Had she ever known how to go about it?

He went on, a stubborn tone to his voice: "So, things are still the same with you?"

Suddenly, Cheranne had only one desire: to get away, back to Omar-Jo and Maxime. She pictured herself seated between the two as she had been a moment ago. She tried to see them through the telephone-booth window.

Her glasses had just slipped down to the end of her nose; the room seemed blurred. She could scarcely make out her two friends; they looked like a single body with two heads. Or, rather, a single mast floating on a quiet, nocturnal sea.

"I have to leave, Steve."

"I'm boring you—well, just come out and say it: I bore you. But what *can* I talk about with you?"

He began to go over and over his grievances again.

"All that has nothing to do with us anymore, Steve. That's over and done with."

She just couldn't get off the line, cut it short. Finally, the receiver slipped from her hands. She left it hanging, turning round at the end of its twisting cord, as she left the booth.

Moving slowly toward the table, several times Cheranne had to resist the temptation to retrace her steps, to pick up the phone again, to resume the interrupted conversation.

Maxime was rising to draw up a chair for her. Cheranne was touched by his round face, his welcoming smile.

"Cheranne, we have a plan for the Merry-go-round," said the child. "You're part of it, if you'll accept."

"I accept," she said.

"Before you know?—"

"I'll like it. I know I'll like it."

Maxime considered putting up a little open-sided tent for their presentation of the show Omar-Jo had dreamed up. With confidence in the dynamism of the child, who had already transformed the Merry-go-round into a unique attraction, the *forain* buried himself in plans and computations, and he set about taking the necessary steps.

Omar-Jo was sure that with the help of Cheranne and Sugar his attractive, unusual show would be a success.

Sugar was twenty-two. Cheranne had come into his nightclub one evening; the young woman's lyrics suited his music; they had been working together for several months.

As soon as he met Omar-Jo, Sugar invited him to his room in a building in the Thirteenth Arrondissement. His window looked out on the roofs of the city; the zinc shingles were a coat of glistening scales on sunny days. The two confided in each other very quickly.

"I was born in New Orleans. My father died when I was nine. It was then that I learned he had two wives and two families. He left me nothing, not even a shoelace."

Sugar fell silent for several moments before continuing: "Some say, 'Nothing'; I say, 'Everything!' He left me 'everything.' My mad love for music, I get it from him. That was my inheritance! Anywhere there was music, my father was at home; and it's the same for me. I'm at home in the music. He used to improvise on the guitar every night. He was never short of inspiration.

"For a while, he owned a Cadillac; he'd stick me in the back and take me everywhere with him. When he played, I adored my father. I'd laugh, I'd cry when I listened to him. When I look at you and listen to you, Omar-Jo, I have the impression that for you, too, laughter and tears are one and the same. It all comes up from the same depths, from the same heart, from the same well.

"As soon as my father stopped playing, he frightened me. He'd fly into a terrible rage whenever he drank, and he drank from the time he woke up in the morning. He was a strange guy! He dyed his hair red and green, he wore sky blue suits and yellow shoes. Often, when he came toward me, I'd take to my heels. Then, when he took up his guitar again, he became a god. I couldn't leave him anymore.

"At his funeral, there wasn't even a casket, not even a gravestone with his name on it. They dumped him straight into the ground. My mother's youth had been worn away by sorrow. Then she disappeared. I never heard anyone speak of her again. What were your parents like, Omar-Jo?"

"Tell me more about yourself, Sugar, I'll tell you about my life a little later."

"After my father's death, I told myself that if there was music in him, then certainly it was in me too. But I didn't want it to come out through the same instrument. I chose the sax. I'm not my father, and yet I come from him: I play as he did, with my heart pounding so hard through all my body that I'm carried away *tout le corps et toute l'âme*— body and soul. It's like making love. Do you understand me, Omar-Jo?"

"I understand you."

Outside, on the roofs, awkward pigeons waddled to the edge of the eaves. They only regained their birdly grace when they spread their wings to fly away.

Sugar filled the child's hand with seeds. "Go on, they're used to it. They're not afraid."

Omar-Jo stepped over the windowsill to the music of Sugar's muted sax.

The pigeons pecked in the palm of the child's hand, settled on his head and shoulders.

The music expressed that image and their meeting, surrounded by the magical radiance that precedes the end of day.

"All I put in my music is the story of my life."

Inside the room, all of one wall was papered with photos.

"Who are they?" asked Omar-Jo, sitting down cross-legged on the floor before the many pictures.

"My idols!"

"Tell me their names."

Sugar's face seemed carved from an ebony ball; there were shining yellow flecks in his black eyes; his lanky body grew longer and longer until it touched the ceiling. The young man pointed at each photo as he stood before it; he scanned one name after another to a tap-dance staccato: "Dizzy Gillespie, Charlie Parker, Cab Calloway, Duke Ellington, Dave Brubeck—this one's my father—Buddy Rich, Louis Armstrong, Billie Holliday, Milt Jackson, Ella Fitzgerald, Nat King Cole—again, another picture of my father —Thelonious Monk, Coltrane, Pharaoh Sanders . . ."

"Pharaoh?" interrupted the child. "Maybe he comes from my own father's—Omar's—country."

"Don't forget to tell me the whole story of your family, Omar-Jo."

"I will—now, Sugar, say the names of your musicians again. Repeat them slowly; I want to learn them all by heart."

He began again, this time with a clap for each syllable. The child, who had stood up again, worked out a few steps, then tap-danced to Sugar's rhythm.

"Tomorrow I'll sing you all those names. From memory!"

"What about you, Omar-Jo?"

The child hesitated.

"No idols at all?" repeated Sugar.

"Yes," he said, thinking it over a minute. "I have one idol. Only one."

"Who is it?" asked Sugar.

"Next time, I'll bring you his photo."

Interrupting their vacation for three days, Antoine and Rosie had come back up to Paris to check on the laundry, which Claudette had taken care of in their absence.

The day after they arrived, they decided to take a walk over to the Merry-go-round.

All the horses were in use; the coach was overflowing with kids. There was a long line near the ticket window. A large crowd squeezed together around the platform.

"That's a booming business!" exclaimed Antoine.

They didn't immediately recognize Omar-Jo, who had traded his Chaplin outfit for his "bee" costume. He was fluttering his wide transparent wings; his face was hidden under silky brown fuzz.

As soon as he sighted his two relatives, he took one jump off the turning platform and hurried in their direction. Rosie stepped backward before his shaggy-furred face. The child always surprised her. Sensing that his cousin was uncomfort-

146   able, Omar-Jo hastily unglued part of his mask and held out a smooth pink cheek. She kissed it.

Adults' and children's voices together called, "Omar-Jo! Omar-Jo, come back! Again, Omar-Jo! Again!" Turning around to his public, the child promised to come back without delay.

As he observed what was going on around him, Antoine regretted, and was even bitter, that he hadn't been able to make a profit from the boy's talents. Omar-Jo would certainly have helped his business. He made a mental calculation of what the *forain* brought in on a single afternoon like this. Multiplying the number of children by the ticket price and by the hours they were open, he came up with a tempting figure.

"Do you have this many people every day?" he asked.

"About the same every day," answered Omar-Jo. "Soon, we'll have a tent with a real show."

"Do you realize," he whispered to his wife as the child went off again, "how many tickets that adds up to? Your intuition let you down, Rosie; you should have kept him from leaving us. With him, our business would have thrived."

"Omar-Jo in a laundry!"

Antoine shrugged his shoulders. The clever kid would get along in anything at all, anywhere. "A laundry, a merry-go-round . . . what's the difference? It's all just business! And as far as making money is concerned, your little cousin is awfully gifted."

Rosie watched the child. His gaiety heightened the others' gaiety. He and the crowd helped each other out, played against each other, back and forth. They were possessed by a common joy.

"Profit's not what it's all about," she slipped in. "Don't you feel that way, Antoine?"

To his way of thinking, his wife's reaction was absurd, childish; he turned away to speak directly to the child, who was approaching once more.

"What do you earn at the Merry-go-round?" he inquired seriously.

"I get my room. I get my meals."

"Right. But that's not what I'm asking. What do you earn? What are you paid for your work?"

"I'm not working. I'm having fun. And I'm giving them some fun too!" He waved his arm toward the people cheering him.

"You're not answering my question," insisted Antoine.

Wagging his wings, leaping, making faces, Omar-Jo was gone again.

Antoine wondered if it wasn't his duty to intervene to protect the interests of this minor whose guardian he was.

Recognizing Rosie and Antoine from a distance, Maxime came over to them.

"Your Omar-Jo has saved my Merry-go-round!" he greeted them.

"I didn't expect all this," said Antoine in admiration.

"When you're back from your vacation, I'll come to see you. I have plans for Omar-Jo," went on the carousel owner.

"I do too. I wanted to talk to you about the child."

"So—come back in September! Soon, we'll put up a small tent; we already have a little team working on the show. I'm taking care of the last formalities. You'll be my guests for the opening."

"I'll invite you first," came in Rosie. "Monsieur Maxime, I'll make a dinner of our specialties just for you. Omar-Jo told me how much you appreciated my cooking, that you ate every last bit. I was glad, Maxime. Really pleased."

SUGAR AND CHERANNE were seated apart from the others, side by side on iron chairs; they were taking notes, working out the details of the coming show.

As soon as Rosie and Antoine went off, Maxime stared at the young woman. He wished that the crowd would disperse, and that then Sugar and Omar-Jo would go away, so he could be alone with her. Would he be able to speak? He was a fellow who used to start up romantic affairs with a few gestures, a few jokes, and now, suddenly, he was timid, stammering when face-to-face with Cheranne.

She had just spotted him and called, "Come here, Maxime! Come and see one of our projects."

"I'll invite a whole lot of people for the night of the opening," announced the *forain*. "The whole family, all Omar-Jo's friends. All my family, too."

He imagined his family's arrival, their amazement. Would they still disagree, still disapprove? Or would they let themselves be persuaded? Maxime was sorry Uncle Leonard wouldn't be there; he had disappeared deep in the dust along with the kite, but he lived again so often in his thoughts.

"You too, Cheranne. You can invite whoever you
want . . ."

He waited for her answer, so he could find out if the young woman had a relationship, ties, with another man. With the man on the telephone, the one she'd conversed with for such a long time the other night in the telephone booth at the brasserie.

But she murmured only, "Thank you, Maxime," then kept her silence.

axime had obtained information about the prosthesis he intended to give Omar-Jo. A bit later, he told him about the appointment he had made with one of the best practitioners.

They caught the bus on a rainy afternoon. The carousel man smiled happily during the drive.

There was a scramble at the stop. Unable to hold himself up with one hand on the rail, Omar-Jo slipped on the steps and landed on the sidewalk. Maxime helped him get up and dust off his clothes.

"You'll see. With the prosthesis, things like that won't happen anymore. You'll be a normal child."

"I *am* a normal child," retorted Omar-Jo, drawing himself up.

Aware of how clumsy he had been, Maxime covered his embarrassment with a flood of words, which didn't stop until they reached the door of the medical office.

The prosthetist tried several prostheses on the child. Maxime insisted on getting the best.

The assistant showed him a model and demonstrated how it hooked together. Then, he extolled its delicate moving parts, its suitability, and marveled at its flesh-colored covering.

"You'd never guess it wasn't real, would you?"

The boy's exposed stump and all these goings-on in front of the child bothered the *forain*. He wanted Omar-Jo fitted with the limb, which would double his dexterity, and that would be the end of it!

"When will it be ready?" he asked.

"We'll take measurements, and in three weeks you can pick it up. You'll see, son. You'll be satisfied with it. With sleeves, nobody will even see it."

"I don't want it."

Clear, categorical, each word articulated, Omar-Jo's voice rang through the waiting room. A long frozen silence followed.

"Pardon me, Uncle Maxime, but I don't want it."

They left the office quickly. Impressed by the boy's reaction, the prosthetist refused to take a fee.

With all his body, with all his being, Omar-Jo had summarily rejected the apparatus, the artificial limb that would have been joined to his mutilated but still living flesh.

The child had gotten used to his stump little by little. Even the sutures, dissolved now in the closed wound, were part of it. He would forget the member momentarily, so that he could continue to exist and to function better. Yet, at the same time, it must always live in him as the representation of an amputation, of a permanent cry. You couldn't trade that arm for another nor betray its image. Its absence was a reminder of all absences, of all deaths, of all sorrows.

For some time now, it seemed that peace had come back over there. But who can swear that the grenade of men's madness wouldn't explode once more?

Yet, you had to live. To live by maintaining human ties and hope.

"You aren't angry?" he asked Maxime on their way back.

"You did the right thing, Omar-Jo. You're yourself. And you're unique. That can't be replaced."

They joined hands. They strolled home the way they liked to: taking an unexpected route, turning into surprising alleyways.

After an hour, a few yards away from the Place Saint-Jacques, they saw the Merry-go-round, jam packed, still turning.

A few days later, Omar-Jo came into Sugar's room holding a large brown envelope in his hand.

"Guess what's inside."

"Your idol!" murmured the black without hesitation.

The child drew the red-cloth-covered pedestal table under the ceiling lamp. With its sliding cord, you could pull the lamp with its white enameled shade right over what you wanted to illuminate.

Omar-Jo placed the envelope under the bright light, then pulled out the photograph slowly, prolonging the wait. First, he presented it face down to build suspense.

A few moments later, he flipped it face up.

In full light, as if in a spotlight, an old man was dancing.

There was old Joseph, dancing.

At the head of his procession, he was all you could see!

His black cotton, long-sleeved, collarless shirt set off his strong shoulders, his broad torso. Loose trousers, Turkish style and of the same black as his shirt, came down tight around his ankles. You could see his feet between the heavy straps of his sandals.

One foot, on point, was fixed to the ground and supported the powerful body. He had drawn up the other foot and held it at a right angle to the vertical leg as he started his pirouette.

One arm was stretched out horizontally. The other, in a vertical position above the dancer's head, raised a curved sword beginning its spiral.

The ceremonial of the dance was about to begin.

In the black-and-white photograph, you could make out the old man's wrinkles, his cracked lips, the tip of his tongue. His eagle profile, his proud mustache made his presence even more imposing.

His passion made the glossy paper glow, pierced time and space, was inscribed within the eternal present.

"That's my grandfather," said Omar-Jo.

"What movement!" exclaimed Sugar. "What movement!"

To feel closer to his grandson, old Joseph decided to make a merry-go-round like the one on the Place Saint-Jacques, which he'd seen in the numerous color photos Omar-Jo had sent him. He would set up the second carousel below his small vineyard, on his own land.

After thirteen years of combat, the country was experiencing a momentary calm, interrupted by occasional skirmishes.

The capital had been split in two so many times, then cut in pieces again—thus multiplying the divisions and conflicts—that the people, tenacious and eager for hope though they were, were wary. They had seen every sort of public figure come to light; they had been subjected to every sort of quarrel. These disputes surfaced again and again, died down, then sprang up once more. Cities or mountains plunged into bloody struggles, fratricides often instigated by exterior forces. In the shadows, drug and arms traffickers prospered, stirring up corruption and disorder, thanks to which they escaped all law and punishment.

The idea that men could abandon themselves to their own extermination drove Joseph mad.

His own village, miraculously spared until now, was a model open community: in spite of relentless conflicts, they lived in solidarity and harmony. The hamlet hadn't suffered on its own soil, in its own stones; yet, somewhere within the small country in which they were trapped, each person had lost a relative, a friend.

Here, every inhabitant had worn mourning for Omar and Annette.

JOSEPH GOT IT into his mind that the idea of the Merry-go-round was a sign, the sign of an end to the cycles of destruction. The turning platform would represent our lives, some rides longer or shorter than others. The players would give up their places to others in a natural succession while the eternal cavalcade under a protective tent would go on in perpetuity.

The old man was grateful that Maxime's Merry-go-round had served as a springboard for Omar-Jo. The child was breathing, developing in a different place, not in memories. He was living in a different way, not in the past, not in antagonisms and in fear. The ghosts of Annette and Omar, perhaps soon Joseph's own ghost, would not hinder but support him.

Joseph imagined his own Merry-go-round streaking through space. He dreamed it: flying over the Mediterranean, rising up over the clouds to pick up speed. He saw it coming down again in sight of the Riviera, then following a line up the middle of France, straight to Paris.

Once there—thanks to the detailed map of the city that the old man consulted, with his finger tracing the routes the child had described in each letter—he would locate Notre-Dame. From there, he would steer expertly toward the Châtelet.

When his own Merry-go-round was finally right above Maxime's, crowning it like a diadem, with a deft maneuver Joseph would stop its flight. There it would float, hover, turn, a few yards above Maxime's Merry-go-round, at the same rhythm and with the same movement. Replicas, aerial or terrestrial, of each other, they would continue their fraternal dance through the years.

Joseph nailed a photograph of Maxime's Merry-go-round, enlarged several times, to the trunk of an ancient olive tree. He referred to it every morning before he set about his work.

He began by leveling a large area of land before putting up the rounded platform that would be his floor. Then, he inserted a thick stake in the middle of the flooring and set fifteen more of them around the first, horizontally; each pole was to have a carved wooden figure attached to the end of it.

Joseph very quickly gave up the idea of making horses, preferring more familiar animals in their place. They were a cock, a mongrel dog, a donkey, a gouty cat, an obese rabbit, a ladybug, a goat, a silkworm—all were of his own making. The coach became a chariot. He added a wheelbarrow, which all the kids could pile into.

The old man handled the hammer and saw extremely well. He knew all the secret skills of using a plane or a drill, used a gouge, a trying plane, a buffer competently.

Wishing to surprise his neighbors once the work was done, Joseph had some young men help him put up a fence of planks and branches around the work site.

All day long and part of the night, he would toil away—tirelessly, it seemed—cutting up tree trunks, trimming, assembling them. He would put in pegs, glue, jigsaw, whistling or listening to the transistor hung around his neck all the while.

The job was coming to an end; there was only one last animal to construct. Joseph decided to make this one an exceptional creature, a magical beast, straight out of his head, that would look like nothing ever seen before. A dream animal, imaginary, with moving eyes. It would have paws, wings, fins—all at the same time—so it could survive anyplace, under any circumstances.

He would give him a nickname that would testify to the bond between his grandson and himself, that would fuse, combine the letters and syllables of their two names, read forward or backward. Old Joseph searched for the right name for a long time.

One night, the fortuitous discovery roused him abruptly from his sleep: he had it! "Josamjo! . . . it'll be Josamjo!" he exclaimed.

Today I'm finishing Josamjo, the one I prefer to all my other animals. Many will wonder if this strange beast truly exists. Only you, Omar-Jo, and I will have the key to that name, in which our combined names will stay linked together forever and ever. You and I will know that Josamjo exists because we have imagined him, made him, willed him to be.

Soon our friends will knock down the fence. That day, I'll give each one a free ride. A stationary one because my own ride has everything a Merry-go-round should have except one: a motor. I'm really a dolt about such things.

After I come to visit you, you will come back here with Maxime, Cheranne, and your pal Sugar for a long vacation, since now the truce is lasting, and they're talking about disarming all the factions soon.

I'll leave you for the present, my boy. Our Josamjo, which I've just finished, is waiting for his paint. I've chosen the most expensive, the most sparkling.

Your own old Joseph

THE OLD MAN had remembered that Nawal's son was a paint seller. He was often remorseful because he had pushed away his former lover so roughly the day Annette and his son-in-law disappeared. He told himself that by ordering cans of paint from the young man, he would have a chance to apologize to Nawal.

As soon as Joseph thought of Nawal, his feelings were ambivalent: sharp nostalgia mixed with quiet exasperation.

Rushdie arrived in his delivery van with his stock of paint. His mother was seated in the driver's seat, immobile, her hands folded over her stomach, trying to remain unnoticed.

Joseph approached, opened the van door, invited her to join her son in the house, where he served them coffee and figs from his garden.

STARTING THE NEXT DAY the old man set about painting Josamjo.

But that day, the very same day, death was to take him by surprise. It showed him some consideration, though. It left him enough time to arrange his five cans of paint around him on the Merry-go-round floor.

Moreover, it allowed him to climb up astride his animal —the coat of the day before had already dried—to spread a first coat on the animal's neck and head, then to brighten up its plumed mane with bold, primary hues.

Death was patient longer still.

It let him put on more coats, carefully, which outlined the edges, accentuated the reliefs.

As the crowning touch, he dipped his brush in a viscous golden liquid; he picked it up, dripping with sunlight. Then, suddenly, a satisfied smile on his lips, the old man collapsed.

It happened without a jolt, without preliminary suffering. Old Joseph had simply crumpled, gently, noiselessly, like a sack of meal, over the damp neck of Josamjo.

Traces of still wet paint were imprinted on his open white shirt and streaked his neck and all his face with gold.

The villagers dressed the cadaver of their poet in his black ceremonial clothes; on his feet, they put sandals, their soles

162 worn through from dancing down rough-stoned paths so often.

Notified by her son, Nawal hurried there for the final washing.

She sobbed, kissing the stiffened hands of the old madman she had never ceased to love.

The priest from the neighboring village, who had rarely seen Joseph at services, but who had known him for a long time, placed his own crucifix on the old man's broad chest.

"The friend of all has his place in this life and in the other," he concluded.

No one could clean off old Joseph's face, remove the last traces of paint. All that gold stuck to his skin.

"An excellent product, imported from Germany," Rushdie murmured to his mother. "Indelible color. Don't wear yourself out; you'll never rub it off."

Thus it was that Joseph entered into the night of his coffin: yellow streaks on his hands, traces of sunlight on his forehead.

I t was autumn. In only a matter of days, the tent would be in place.

Maxime had ordered a dark blue suit and an opera hat
in anticipation of the opening. He would be the announcer
of the coming show; Cheranne and Omar-Jo had prepared
his speech.

At the moment, the child, dressed in his suit of lights
with its feather and garland decorations, was prancing
around the moving platform.

Suddenly, he stopped, as if knifed in the back. He pivoted, staggered. His muscles gave way. He had to lean back
against the coach to hold himself up.

Cheranne, who had been watching his movements,
called to the *forain*, "Maxime come quickly—Omar-Jo's not
well."

Used to the boy's abrupt changes of mood, the carousel
man shrugged his shoulders. "No reason to be upset. That's
all just part of his act."

"Not this time, Maxime. Look at him."

The child's face was ashen; his body trembled. Not a sound came from his throat. Even the audience, which had been applauding him a few seconds earlier, fell silent, ill at ease.

"Something strange is going on, I'm sure," insisted Cheranne. "Go see, Maxime."

The *forain* approached as the music died away, as the platform stopped turning.

The disoriented children didn't know what to do anymore: to stay where they were or to go back to their parents.

His hands cupped around his mouth, Maxime whispered, "Don't you think you're overdoing it, Omar-Jo? This time, you've got everyone upset with your buffoonery."

Making an effort to turn toward Maxime, the child gave him a pleading look. "Come get me, Uncle Max. I'm not playing now. I swear I can't move anymore . . ."

The child's face had grown even paler; his arms and legs were shaking.

The *forain* lifted him up, bore him away in his arms; he hesitated for a moment, his heart thumping. Then he went toward the booth to wait for the return of Cheranne, who had run to get help.

It was the next day that Maxime received a telegram announcing old Joseph's disappearance. He didn't feel it necessary to notify the child, convinced as he was that Omar-Jo already knew.

The great celebration was being organized; it was to take place soon.

Cheranne was preparing her songs; Sugar, his music. In rehearsals, the two of them moved smoothly and gracefully. Although they gave the impression they were improvising, as they moved over the floor in a dance of the planets, their steps were precise, codified, each in harmony with the others.

Omar-Jo was adding some sketches to his clown acts. He was able to perform more difficult acrobatic feats as his body grew more and more agile; his face, more and more expressive, would slip constantly from candor to lucidity, from purity to desolation. His tongue, more and more glib, invented flower-words, whip-words, lightning-words, captive-words.

Maxine was learning his announcements by heart. Exercising his voice, he was surprised to discover that it had timbre and range.

The lanterns would flicker until dawn around the Merry-go-round and its tent on the night of the opening. They had the permits. Clouds of smoke, blue and pink, would rise from the corners of the small garden, then would be pushed aside by frequent flights of many-colored balloons.

After the show, friends and family would attend a reception in a reserved room at the Brasserie des Trois Portes. At the end of the meal, a glass of champagne in his hand, surrounded by confetti and applause, Maxime would rise. He would begin by saying, "To you, Omar-Jo. First and foremost, to you!" Then, he would go on, expressing just how he felt. Finally, in conclusion, he would make a surprise announcement to all those gathered there.

"After the party, I shall make a public announcement. A surprise!"

Maxime couldn't help talking about it.

"What surprise?" asked Cheranne.

"A surprise for all of you. Especially for you, Omar-Jo."

"For me? . . . what, Uncle Max?"

"That's my secret. If I told you, it wouldn't be a surprise anymore."

Since that conversation, Maxime had spent every Sunday completely absorbed in a mysterious dossier.

"Paperwork. These damned forms to fill out," he would mutter as he scribbled in the margins.

The child's presence, his constant coming and going in the two-room apartment irritated him.

"Go take a walk, Omar-Jo!"

"What's got you in such a foul mood, Uncle Max? Fees, taxes?"

"That's the way it is in our civilized countries. Take it or leave it. Everything has to be in writing . . . in your land," he went on sarcastically, "I don't suppose you even pay taxes!"

"Possibly. My country's in shambles."

"Okay. Fine. Now let me do my work."

The child went on, unflustered: "My ancestors on my father's side invented red tape. They were called 'a nation of scribes.' They inscribed everything on rolls of papyrus. There are lots and lots of them left. On my mother's side, there were the discoverers of the alphabet. It was on the sarcophagus of Ahirim . . ."

"What are you going on about!" Maxime cut in. "Did I ask you for a lecture on antiquity?"

"You mentioned 'civilization,' didn't you?"

"I get it, Omar-Jo. I've piqued your precious self-esteem again. So, to get back at me, you throw your tombs and your pharaohs in my face."

"We're even, Uncle Max?"

Maxime burst out laughing. "We're even, you darn kid."

"I'M TURNING the Merry-go-round over to you for the day," Maxime notified him a week later.

"The whole day without you?"

"I'll come by for you this evening, around six. We'll go home together as usual."

That afternoon, Cheranne was surprised to find that Maxime was not around.

"It's his wonderful secret again!" said the child.

The young woman had given lengthy consideration to that surprise, of which Maxime planned to make a formal announcement. It could only be about his coming marriage, she reflected; the *forain* was waiting for an opportunity to present his young wife, hidden away discreetly someplace until the evening when they would all be together.

Just thinking about it, Cheranne felt something akin to pain, a burning in the back of her throat. Had she tried to ignore what she was beginning to feel? Feelings constantly held in check by the passion that tied her to Steve?

There had been no sign of life from Steve for more than a month; she was no longer sure if his silences were good for her or not. Throughout her life, she had gone through phases of acute distress and peace, periods when she was stable or shaky.

To make a living, Cheranne continued to take children on outings or act as a companion to elderly ladies during the day. The day before, thanks to Sugar, she had had an audition with the manager of his club, who had listened to her songs and liked them. He quickly engaged her to sing them twice a week, after midnight. She was to begin the following day.

"Maxime will be back at six," the child confirmed.

"I'll wait with you."

At six, Maxime hadn't reappeared. Not at seven, nor at eight.

His prolonged absence confirmed Cheranne's suspicions.

"Maybe he's been to see his 'secret,'" she said casually, in a disinterested tone.

They went on waiting.

Shorter now, the days were growing cooler. The crowd had disappeared quite awhile ago. The garden had been swallowed up by darkness.

The time had come to cover up the Merry-go-round with its heavy tarp; Sugar had arrived just in time to help them with it.

After that, it was nine o'clock. Soon, ten. And then, eleven.

The young saxophonist had to leave for the cabaret. "I'll come back tomorrow for news."

"He's having a fine evening. And he's forgotten all about us!" Cheranne spoke again.

"That can't be it," replied the child.

He was beginning to worry, but he tried hard not to let it overwhelm him. Omar-Jo had the impression that if he gave in to fear, he would arouse fear in the young woman. Who knows if it wouldn't even reach Maxime, who, perhaps at this very instant, needed all the strength he had to face difficulties or a real danger?

"Let's go check his apartment," said the child in a confident voice. "I must have misunderstood; it must be he's waiting for us at his house."

Maxime was not at home.

They both searched in vain for signs of where he might have gone.

The modest building had no watchman. They went down to the street, questioned a newspaper vendor whose

170   kiosk stayed open late. From her observation post, she kept track of the comings and goings of her usual clients with a curious, familiar eye.

She hadn't seen Maxime. She couldn't have missed him; if he didn't buy a paper, he always said hello in passing.

"What's happened to him? An accident?"

Face-to-face with headlines for more than forty years, the vendor moved in a world of catastrophes. Convinced that calamities could come into anybody's life from one day to the next, she repeated, "Good Lord! Maxime's been in an accident."

Without responding, Cheranne and Omar-Jo left immediately.

All night long, together, in one police station or hospital after another, they searched for the *forain.*

It was only in the early morning hours that they learned that Maxime, slightly intoxicated, had been hit by a car coming up out of one of the tunnels at the Place de la Concorde.

Omar-Jo and Cheranne discovered him in the intensive care ward. He was stretched out, strapped down on a mattress covered with transparent plastic. Tubes came from his nose; others, from his limbs, his chest. His coloring leaden, dark shadows around his closed eyes, he was gasping for air. The pallid flesh of his shoulders was exposed.

Maxime was but a body in extremis that held fast, animal-like, to what breath it had left. It rose to his lips in intermittent flurries, was spent, then began again, as if pushed forth by some invisible motor.

"At first, the poor man was delirious," confided the nurse. "He called out continually, 'Chaplin, Chaplin! You know, Charlie Chaplin.' After that, he slipped into a coma."

Relegated to his narrow battleground, to the cramped boxing ring of his bed, the *forain* struggled fitfully to thwart

172 death's assault. At times, his feet moved, thrashed about, as if he were trying to flee danger, to run away. At other times, his face assumed a fierce, belligerent look, as if he were getting ready to get into the fight, to meet his adversary head on in violent hand-to-hand combat.

Then, suddenly, totally exhausted, the patient would let go and withdraw into himself, giving all the advantage to his powerful enemy.

THE DAY BEFORE, a bottle of champagne under his arm, Maxime had been hit broadside by a car. It had dragged him several yards down the road. Luckily, by pumping their brakes, other drivers just missed him.

The ambulance attendants found the carousel owner lying in a pool of red. The thick, heavy blood on the ground was mixed with floating aromatic bubbles leaking from the shattered bottle.

STANDING at the foot of the bed, leaning against the railing, Omar-Jo didn't take his eyes off his friend.

This time, it was too much! Ever since his birth, death had relentlessly hunted down Omar-Jo and those he loved. In the end, it always caught up with them and brought them to defeat.

This time, he wouldn't take it! This time, death hadn't come along by accident. It had announced itself. Omar-Jo had had the time to recognize it, to tear off its mask, and now to meet it face-to-face.

An insuppressible energy came to Omar-Jo. In the evening, he refused to leave the hospital. Convinced that the *forain* was living his last hours, the personnel let the child stay at his side.

When Cheranne had left, Omar-Jo came close to Maxime and spoke to him in a hushed voice: "Hold on, Uncle Max. I need you. We all need you: Cheranne, Sugar, me, the others. Hold on, you're going to recover. I won't let you get an inch away from me. Together, you and I will win."

By all the means available to him, the child tried to reach Maxime, to get inside his locked world. By his voice, by physical contact, he tried to slip inside the straitjacket of the grievously stricken body; he tried to cut his way into that closed flesh by his words and his touch.

"Hold on, Uncle Max. Hold on."

He repeated those same words, placed his palm on his friend's forehead, on his shoulders, caressed the backs of his hands.

"I won't leave here without you. You know how I am—mule headed."

At dawn, after a very long night, Omar-Jo caught a slight flicker of Max's eyelids, then, later, a puckering of his lips. He told the nurse, who alerted the aide.

Later, inarticulate sounds rose in his throat. His breathing grew less ragged.

Two days later, Maxime left the intensive care ward for a hospital room.

It was as he was going into that sunny room—stretched out on a gurney pushed by an attendant—that Maxime caught sight of a large splash of red that filled the whole corner of the room.

"The Poppy Woman!" were his first words.

The child was hollow cheeked. His huge eyes, shining as never before, filled his entire face.

The *forain* called him, "Come here, Omar-Jo."

In one leap, he rose from the chair where he had dropped and hurried to his friend.

"Closer . . ."

The injured man tossed about, opened his mouth several times, but there was no sound from his lips.

"Don't speak yet, Uncle Max. You shouldn't get too tired."

The carousel owner shivered, struggled, as if what he had to say wouldn't wait.

"Closer," suggested Cheranne.

The child lowered his head until his ear brushed Maxime's lips.

"The surprise, Omar-Jo, the secret . . . ," he articulated.

He caught his breath and declared in an uninterrupted rush of words, "Now your name is Omar-Jo Chaplin Lineau . . . Lineau, like me."

"That rhymes," said the child, at a loss for words.

"That rhymes, and I'm adopting you . . . all the papers are signed."

He tried to add, "The champagne . . . was for . . ."

But the nurse, who had just come in, frowned and insisted he calm down.

As soon as she had left, Maxime called the child again, "Just one word . . . a single word."

"Just one. That's a promise?"

"A promise."

"Well, I'm listening."

"All that's gratis,'" he murmured. "Gratis!"

"Gratis!" the child said again, as though they had just given each other a password.

"Gratis, gratis, gratis," he repeated as he twirled around the bed on tiptoe. For the first time since the accident, the *forain* smiled.

THAT DAY, Cheranne was carefully groomed.

The day before, Steve had reappeared; he would stay in Paris a full week. She was going to meet him in a restaurant near the Étoile when she left the hospital.

Never had Cheranne looked so attractive, so radiant. Maxime noticed that her hair was shorter; she had replaced her glasses with contact lenses. The air was fragrant with her fresh, crisp perfume.

"Tonight, it's my turn to take your place here," she said to Omar-Jo, suddenly changing her plans.

She passed along the bed, came closer, placed a kiss on Maxime's forehead. Then, gently, she ran her fingers through his hair.

"I'll spend the night with you, Maxime."

He tried, unconvincingly, to protest.

"Don't say a thing, it's all decided. I want to stay close to you."

"When I was going home . . . I recognized your color . . . ," he uttered with difficulty.

"My poppy dress! I know you like it."

She decided to lie: "I put it on just for you, Maxime."

As she voiced those words, they suddenly seemed true to her, sincere.

In a little while, she would telephone Steve and find some excuse. Perhaps they would put off their meeting until the next day or some other day? Perhaps they wouldn't see each other anymore? She hesitated for a moment, felt the urge to run to him; but it was too late to reconsider her decision.

SUGAR, who went by the hospital for news every day had come back—late that night, after his number—to hang around the Merry-go-round. There, he found Omar-Jo.

As soon as the latter announced that the carousel owner was out of danger, they agreed to get busy. First, they tore up the poster that announced the cancellation of the show and the reduction in the Merry-go-round's hours of operation because of an accident, replacing it with a sign that set the opening for a later date and the return to regular hours of their shows.

It was after two A.M. To celebrate the *forain*'s return, the two of them took off the tarp, lit the lanterns, set the platform in motion.

Then, without consultation, one dancing, the other playing his sax, they went around the Merry-go-round and the garden.

The moon didn't show up. But what did it matter!

Sugar and Omar-Jo played and danced for all that is darkness in the world, for all that is light. For all the Maximes, the Josephs, the Omars; for all the Annettes, the Cherannes. For all friends, known and unknown, who people the planet. For all those whom life favors and all it treats so cruelly. For all the hours to come, which we must always, endlessly, bring to life again.

Omar-Jo and Sugar went on dancing, playing, giving rhythm to the night; they swung back and forth to the same beat, stayed in place, pranced about.

While a few night strollers came into the square to listen and to look at them, fine drops of rain began to fall.

Winter was near.

All sped toward the cold, toward violence, toward death. All fled toward summer, toward peace, toward life. Turning, twirling without end, the Merry-go-round still went round.

Of Lebanese descent, ANDRÉE CHEDID was born in Cairo in 1920. After publishing a book of verse, *On the Trails*, written in English, she moved to France in 1946, and since then this prolific novelist, poet, and dramatist has written in French. Her works have been translated into nine languages. In 1994, she won the Prix Paul-Morand, a major French literary prize awarded by the Académie Française. She has also won Morocco's Prix Hassan II, the Prix Louise Labé, the Aigle d'Or de la Poésie, the Grand Prix des Lettres of the Académie Royale de Belgique, the Prix de l'Académie Mallarmé, and the Prix Goncourt de la Nouvelle. Her works in English include *From Sleep Unbound*, *The Prose and Poetry of Andrée Chedid*, and *The Return to Beirut*.

JUDITH RADKE has taught French literature at Arizona State University for many years. Her translations of stories by Andrée Chedid have appeared in various magazines.